LUPO

AND THE THIEF AT THE TOWER OF LONDON

LUPO

AND THE THIEF AT THE TOWER OF LONDON

ABY KING

Illustrated by Sam Usher

Hodder
Children's
Books

A Catalogue record for this book is available from the British Library

ISBN: 978 1 444 92155 7

Typeset in Egyptian 505 BT Light by Avon DataSet Ltd,
Bidford-on-Avon, Warwickshire

Printed and bound by Clays Ltd, St Ives plc

MIX
Paper from
responsible sources
FSC® C104740

The paper and board used in this book are made from wood from responsible sources.

Hodder Children's Books
An imprint of Hachette Children's Group
Carmelite House
50 Victoria Embankment
London EC4Y 0DZ

www.hachette.co.uk
www.theadventuresoflupo.com

Thanks for inspiring me through the darkness
of the Tower of London!
This book is for you with love and thanks.

Natalie, Alice and Grace Livingstone
Hannah Shanks-Weston
Caitlin Lomas
Vicky Field
Sean Curry

Contents

Prologue

The thief turned the key and the door opened easily. As he slipped into the Jewel House at the Tower of London, tiny lights automatically turned on inside the cabinets. He waited a few minutes to enjoy the place all to himself before the others arrived to carry out the booty.

Crowns, silverware, clothes and royal orbs waited for his loving attention. He almost lost his breath as thousands of jewels twinkled, celebrating their place within the richly-adorned royal regalia. He cast his gaze over the objects in search of the one he most desired.

"*Twinkle, twinkle little star . . .*" sung the thief as he opened the snakeskin getaway bags below each of the cabinets. "*How I wonder where you are . . .*"

WHACK, WHAM, CRACK sounded the hammer as he broke through the glass.

SMASH! went the first cabinet containing beautiful handmade shields and swords. Broken glass, wood and smart velvet cushions fell to the floor.

CRASH! went the second cabinet, which housed the world's finest collection of royal sceptres, bracelets and robes.

BANG! went the huge iron doors as the thief broke through to the main safe.

The thief took a moment to study the contents. "The crowns of every sovereign past and present. Over there – the crowns of consorts and – up there – the crowns of princes. ALL MINE for the taking. But where are you? Where are you hiding, little star?" he said ominously.

In the corner of the room was a single glass cabinet. Within it was the Imperial State Crown. Made up of over three thousand priceless gems, including the Second Star of Africa, hundreds of pearls, the St Edward's Sapphire, five large rubies and nearly a dozen emeralds. The exquisitely crafted crown rested on top of a purple velvet cap with an ermine border. This was what the thief had come for.

The minute he spotted it he tingled with anticipation.

"*Up above the world so high, like a diamond in the sky . . .*" he sang as he lifted it out of the case and off the velvet cushion, ignoring the alarms that screamed for attention.

The thief pulled the Second Star of Africa off the crown. "Just checking you are a *real* little star and not some human's idea of a joke!" He bit down on to the diamond hard and managed to crack a tooth. It fell to the floor and beneath the broken cabinet. "OUCH!" he yelped.

There wasn't much time left – the police would be arriving any moment. He needed to hurry.

Shaking off the pain of the broken tooth he said aloud, "And now for a bit of cleaning up." He threw the contents of the Jewel House into the snakeskin bags, being careful to leave the precious Imperial State Crown till last.

He signalled for the others, and his group of accomplices burst into the Jewel House. The thief ordered half of them to remove the bags and the other half to "DESTROY THE PLACE. LEAVE NOTHING BUT DESTRUCTION!"

1
Mission: Wake Up, Lupo

It was just after midnight when the little brown mouse appeared in the doorway of the pretty royal nursery at Kensington Palace. The night-light bathed the entire room in a warm, comforting glow. He hurried inside, then ran like a speeding bullet over and under and once around the toys that were littering the carpet. He scurried along the side of Prince George's royal bed and down the back of Princess Charlotte's cot. Herbert, the Head of Mice Intelligence Section 5, was on a mission. He had an important message for Lupo, the royal dog.

The Duke and Duchess's black spaniel was fast asleep under Prince George's bed. Herbert quickly got to work, trying to find Lupo's long, soft black ear, which was artfully hidden amongst a thick mass of fur and paws. At last he found Lupo's nose and quickly climbed on top of it, following it all the way to the edge of the furry ear. It took all his might to lift the heavy black flap and crawl in. Once inside he stood perfectly still, then cleared his throat, ready to deliver an important message. The little mouse took one enormously big breath (for a mouse) and shouted into Lupo's ear.

Lupo didn't move.

Herbert was not beaten. It was of the utmost urgency that Lupo was informed of the situation. Smoothing down his little green cardigan, Herbert tried again. This time he shouted so loudly he knocked his horn-rimmed spectacles right off his face!

At first there was a loud sniff, then Herbert felt a rumbling and then air stirred all around him. Yelling his goodbyes, he squeezed between a tiny gap in the thick wooden floorboards and promised to be back the minute there was more news. The Head of Mice Intelligence Section 5 had completed his mission!

Lupo was quite dazed and more than a little bit confused. The shock of having Herbert shouting down his ear was bad enough but the news which

Herbert had woken him with was even more alarming. He shook himself awake, trying to take the message in. Could it really be true? Lupo wondered if it was even possible.

Both Prince George and Princess Charlotte had been restless for most of the night. None of the royal household had got much sleep. Lupo himself was sleepy. He yawned and stretched, then crawled out from under the Prince's little bed.

Looking over to the window, he could see it was still dark outside. He carefully crept towards the door, hoping not to wake the Duke, who was snoring heavily under a soft baby blanket on the small blue sofa, his long arms and legs dangling all around it. The Duchess was curled up in her dressing gown, sleeping in a large white rocking chair near the door. Lupo padded past hoping not to stir either of them. He already knew that all the royal families would have their sleep disturbed soon. He knew someone would be coming to wake everyone up. All he could do was wait for the knock at the door of Apartment 1A, Kensington Palace, Kensington Gardens, London W8.

He walked into the kitchen and stood for a

moment, listening to the wind and the rain lashing against the palace windows. Resisting the urge to bark, he sat, aiming his gaze at the front door. He didn't have to wait long.

Knock-Knock-Knock. Lupo barked loudly to announce the visitor's arrival.

The Duke was the first to make it to the door. He was all fingers and thumbs, struggling to tie up his old navy dressing gown. On his left foot he was wearing one of the Duchess's slippers and on his right foot he had put on an old, well-chewed slipper. Lupo looked at it lovingly. It was his favourite toy.

"Yes, yes? What is it? What's wrong?" questioned the sleepy Duke, whilst opening the door to the extremely wet police officer.

The Duchess was more composed. She handed the policeman a towel, as he was dripping all over her kitchen floor. Next she offered her husband his other slipper and pointed to her own. "Swap please, darling." Then, smiling at the officer and winking at Lupo, she said in a soft whisper, "I'm hoping all this fuss hasn't woken the children." Turning back to the policeman, she said, "Good evening officer, is everything OK? It's very late."

Kitty the palace tabby cat meowed loudly. This was no way to be woken. Barking, knocking at the door! "Whatever next?" she said to herself as she leapt down off the kitchen worktop, landing between the Duchess and Lupo. Rubbing up alongside him she purred, "Lupo, I know you already know what's going on. If it's bad news I want you to nod."

Lupo looked his tabby friend in the eye and then nodded slowly.

Thanking the kind Duchess, the police officer put down the towel and began. "Please excuse me, your Highnesses, only I thought it best to tell you straight away."

The Duchess reached for her husband's arm. "What is it? What on earth's the matter?"

"There's been a robbery, a rather large one and they have taken . . . well, *everything*," said the flabbergasted officer.

The Duke was immediately worried. "A robbery? Where?"

"In the Jewel House at the Tower, Sir."

"The Tower of London?" asked the Duchess, bewildered and concerned.

"Yes, Your Royal Highnesses, the Tower of London."

Kitty asked Lupo in a series of short meows, "But isn't that where the crown jewels are?"

Before Lupo could answer the palace cat, the officer said, "It's all gone. They have taken the lot."

The Duke suddenly looked a lot more awake. He stared at the officer wide-eyed. "Officer, are you telling us that someone has stolen the crown jewels?!"

"Yes," answered the young man.

The Duke was in shock. "Someone has stolen the crown jewels . . . someone has broken into the Jewel House and stolen everything? It can't be!"

The Duchess helped her husband to a chair and, visibly pale herself, asked, "I don't understand, how can anyone steal the crown jewels? They've been locked up at the Tower of London for hundreds of years and well . . . Who? How?" She sat down next to her deeply concerned husband.

"When?" added the Duke.

"Your Highnesses, we are processing the crime scene now. Unfortunately I am unable to tell you any more at this time." The officer stood up straight and proclaimed with a very pointed finger, "We are doing all we can to catch the perpetrators of this act of treachery against the crown!"

Lupo had heard enough. "Kitty, we have to help."

Kitty's tail was flicking from side to side on the floor. "What exactly are you suggesting we do about it? A palace pooch and a tubby tabby cat: how are we going to help? You heard the man – the finest police force in the world will do their thing and all will be well. I mean, how bad can it be? A few posh jewels disappear – probably nabbed by an over-zealous tourist. I'm going back to bed. Mark my words, this is a fly in the honey pot, a lot of fuss for nothing. Nighty night!"

Lupo's normally soft brown eyes now grew narrow, and his black fur prickled all over. He gripped the floor with his carefully clipped claws. "Kitty, this *is* something. It's bad. I can feel it. We need to go."

"Go? Go where?" said Kitty. "It's the middle of the night! And it's raining. Cats don't go out in the rain. Besides George's uncle is away on a mission to Africa." Lupo looked blankly back, but Kitty was not about to fall for the princely pup's pleading brown eyes. "Don't you know what that means? No, Mr-I-get-to-sleep-in-the-royal-nursery!

It means *I* get a royal bed too! Yes, while he's charging around with rhinos and giraffes, I get the entire bed to roll around on." She added, smirking with pleasure, "All night!"

Lupo had heard enough excuses from the palace cat. "And you get to roll around on it all day, too! Look, come and check this out with me. If it's nothing, I promise to let you sleep tomorrow. I will even steer clear of your milk. But if I'm right and something is going on, you and I can try and put a stop to it."

Kitty wasn't in the least bit interested. She looked out of the window as the trees bent over sideways in the stormy night, and shuddered at the thought of going outside.

Lupo could see her mind was nearly made up. He tried one last time. "Kitty, someone has stolen the palace jewels. This is very bad. Whoever has them has the Queen's crown."

2
A Pantry Pow Wow

Lupo's train of thought was broken by Herbert, who reappeared between the toaster and bread bin. The intelligent mouse took a moment, then he signalled to Lupo and Kitty and bounced towards the pantry. The palace dog and cat followed, leaving the Duke and the officer talking.

The Duchess put the kettle on. "It's going to be a long night," she said, getting three mugs out of the cupboard. "I think everyone could do with a good cup of tea."

Squeezing into the cramped pantry, Herbert found himself surrounded by spiders. "Evening, master Herbert. It must be important for you to be here so late," said Mrs Spider, dropping down and stopping right above his oversized brown ears.

A pack of baby spiders hung on to her long silky threads. Their young faces eyed the group of important visitors.

Being the biggest, Lupo made room for everyone else by sitting down between a bag of rice and a tray of tinned baked beans at the back. Kitty wasn't the slightest bit interested in what Herbert had to say but hated being left out of anything. She remained by the door, licking her paws.

"Tell me you have something more than '*There is a thief at the Tower*'?" questioned Lupo.

"At this point, no, I don't." Herbert shook his head. The mouse saw a look of curiosity in Lupo's eyes. That meant one thing. "I know you, Lupo. This isn't the time for adventures. Listen to me – as a friend and your teacher, I advise you that this is not something you can get yourself tangled up in." Herbert brushed aside a friendly baby spider who was beginning its first web in his green cardigan pocket. "The Tower of London is not to be trifled with. There are things that happen there—" Herbert stopped himself from saying more.

Lupo's mind was made up. "Herbert, I have to protect my family."

Herbert shifted uncomfortably. "I understand. But, Lupo, there are strange reports of animal ghosts and all sorts at the Tower of London. I'm telling you – trust me – this is a human matter."

Lupo grew inquisitive. "What animal ghosts? We've never discussed the Tower's animals before. I know you Herbert, you wouldn't warn me against going to the Tower – unless you thought that animals may have played some kind of role in the robbery."

Herbert shrugged, unable to hide his top-secret knowledge of the crime scene at the Tower's famous Jewel House.

"Herbert, I know you know more than you are letting on. This isn't just a matter for the humans!" said Lupo, knocking a tin of baked beans on to the floor in frustration. It rolled over to Kitty, who put her paws down in front of the tin and stretched. Arching her back, and flicking her tail, she managed to send a thick thread of baby spiders flying with joy around and around the pantry. As they twisted, they whooped. Kitty stood taller. "What he won't tell you, Lupo, is that the animals that go to the Tower never come back. They disappear down the Black route, never to be seen again."

Lupo knew about all the routes beneath Kensington that could take him to any of the royal palaces but no one had ever told him about a Black route. "Herbert, is it true? Is there a Black route to the Tower?"

Herbert was busy pushing the tin of beans back towards Lupo. "Kitty, I thought I told you – no more exploring without my say so. You cats! You have to know everything, don't you? Lupo, the Black route is not somewhere you need to be going. It's very old and very dangerous and we have limited surveillance down there . . . I must insist . . ."

Seeing the uneasy look on Lupo's face, Kitty interrupted gleefully, "Actually, Mr MI5, I'll have you know I've not been near that route. No need.

I get all the information I need from those busy little mice of yours that scurry around Kensington Palace." Herbert looked annoyed. Kitty bent forwards so her whiskers were almost tickling his. "And I'm betting that somewhere in his beloved HQ he has a report on a great big beasty that, legend says, has a monster army. Oh yes, Herbert. I hear your agents whispering all kinds of useful information, even something about an army of slippery, sharp, evil things that destroy anyone who dares travel along the Black route. Isn't that right, Herbie? Isn't that why you don't want anyone using it? Secrets, secrets . . ."

Herbert humped. "I haven't been called Herbie since I was a wee small scamp of a thing. My name is Herbert and Kitty, you know nothing about MI5 HQ. Long may it stay that way!"

Having finished ticking off the palace cat, he walked up to Lupo's nose. "But I'm afraid to say, she's quite right. I didn't mention it before because I knew you would want to go and investigate! There *is* something at the Tower. In fact, there are a few nasty animals and a pretty large collection of animal ghosts." Herbert shuddered. "They're led by a ghostly lion called Nero. He and some of the ghostly animals were part of England's first zoo. They don't seem to be unfriendly but you wouldn't catch me too close to them. Never really liked animal ghosts. The other animals that we think must be stuck down there are the ghosts of animals that strayed too close and got captured by whatever lurks in the shadows. Though the ghosts aren't the problem. There *is* something down there and its heart is as cold and old as the Tower itself."

Lupo was shocked. "Come on, Herbert, how bad can it be? We survived the secret of Windsor Castle and a curse at Buckingham Palace!"

"No, Lupo, this isn't the same. Whatever this creature is, it's vicious and knows what it's doing. One whiff of you and you could very well be just like the others – a ghostly dog destined to spend all eternity floating along the spooky Black route. Trust me – we don't want to be messing with this particular beast."

Kitty had resumed cleaning herself. Taking her paw out of her mouth momentarily, she said, "Herbert, you're scared of ghosts? HA! NOW, that's a first! You should listen to him, Lupo . . . you and your nose for trouble. HA! Knowing your luck, you could end up losing your head like that Anne Boleyn.

Now, that would make headline news! ROYAL DOG GETS HEAD CHOPPED OFF BY OLD BEASTY AND BECOMES ANIMAL GHOST!"

Lupo smiled crookedly at Kitty's joke.

Herbert bounced up to Kitty and, with his hands on his hips, spoke. "That's enough, Kitty!"

Lupo couldn't explain it but he just knew something wasn't right. "Herbert, I am not afraid of a few ghost stories or Kitty's taunting. Besides, didn't you always tell me to look what you are afraid of in the face instead of running from it?" Lupo watched as the mouse lowered his head. "I know you have half a dozen of your top mice agents compiling a report on the robbery as we speak! Those very same mice will be busy interviewing every bat, beetle, buzzard and blue-fly at the Tower – someone must have seen and heard something."

Herbert raised his head and ran his paws over his ears. Lupo was the finest royal student he had ever had. He eyed the royal dog with pride because the spaniel was right, of course.

Lupo continued. "I'm the royal spaniel and tonight someone has decided to steal from my family. I want answers." He stood, signalling that he'd made up his mind. He was going to investigate with or without his friend's help. "And one more thing . . . no one just *decides* to steal the crown jewels on a whim. This was planned and I'm going to find out who did it. Why they took everything and what they want it all for."

Herbert pleaded with Lupo. "Animals wouldn't steal the jewels. It makes no sense. We have no use for gold and such. There really isn't much we can do to help." Herbert added, "I know you want to protect your family, but Lupo, really, there is nothing for you to worry about at this stage. We don't even have a suspect."

Lupo spoke in a whisper, "There's one animal who would find a way to benefit from a robbery of this kind. Vulcan." Lupo saw Kitty shudder.

She grimaced. "Oh please! Vulcan is the Queen's dog, not some beastie. Besides, he couldn't whip up cream let alone an army! Herbert's right. Let the humans sort this mess out for a change. Never understood why we have to get involved. Sure humans aren't exactly clever but can't they, for just this once, capture a thief without us doing all the work?" She yawned loudly. "I'm going to bed.

All this excitement has completely worn me out."

From the pantry, Lupo could hear that both the royal children had woken up. He knew they would never get back to sleep unless he was in the room. "Herbert, I am telling you, the robbery doesn't feel right. I won't do anything until I hear back from you but please look into it and brief me the minute you have an update."

Herbert sighed heavily. "Lupo, you are the best of all the royal dogs. Vulcan has indeed proven himself to be more than troublesome in the past so I'll look into his comings and goings of late. Bernie, the mouse Head of House at Buckingham Palace, keeps a log. If there is anything odd, it will be in the log. I'll be back if my agents have news of anything out of the ordinary."

Lupo thanked his friends and Mrs Spider for the use of her pantry. He walked back into the kitchen and nudged the Duchess's hand with his soft, black nose in a way that told her the children needed her. The Duke poured himself a second cup of tea and shuffled his feet under the table. Lupo pawed at the damaged slipper. There was no time for games tonight. Somewhere deep inside him, something told him that he was headed into particularly dark and murky waters and it would be some time before he would feel happy playing innocently with the children or his slipper again.

3
A Good Night's Sleep

Lupo walked into the nursery to find Prince George and his wombat both wrapped up in sheets, running around the nursery, pretending to be a ghost, much to the amusement of the Prince's baby sister.

"George, back into bed. It's not playtime," said the Duchess, trying not to laugh as his tiny little face beamed up at her.

George giggled, stumbling and tripping over his sheets, as he rushed to get back into bed. "Dodo whooooo."

Lupo translated his toddler talk as, "Lupo, I'm going to be a ghost this Halloween!"

The Duchess smiled. "Very spooky, darling. Now, come on into bed, before Nanny gets here – she won't be pleased when she sees the state of this

23

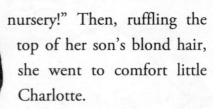

nursery!" Then, ruffling the top of her son's blond hair, she went to comfort little Charlotte.

Lupo pounced on to the bed and whispered into his best friend's ear in the secret language only George and he could understand. "Someone broke into the Tower of London and I need to investigate it."

George gurgled and waved his arms around, and his brown eyes grew bigger – Lupo saw the excitement twinkle in them. Lupo perfectly understood the little boy's toddler talk. "*AD-DENTURE DODO!*"

Lupo helped him tuck his wombat into a pillow, then *sniffed* and *winked* at George. "It seems that way."

"*Wombat help!*" said the brave toddler prince.

Scratching at the sheets, Lupo replied, "I need you to keep a look out here. You can be my eyes and ears. I want you to make a note of anything odd that happens."

George nodded. He was more animated and clearly had no intention of settling down to sleep. He kicked his sheets and pulled at Lupo's long ears. The young toddler wanted to know if he would be going down to the animal city under Buckingham Palace – the City of Creatures. They had made up a story about the City of Creatures after their last adventure at Buckingham Palace. Both of them longed to meet some of the animals that lived under London's most famous palace.

Lupo managed to translate a few of the questions. He *chomped*, "Maybe. I'll tell you all about it when I get back. You promise not to tease your baby sister, OK?" George looked mischievous as he winked back at the spaniel. Lupo smiled and licked the side of the prince's soft cheek. "You'll try. That's enough for me."

"*Holly?*" whispered the prince.

Lupo knew he was asking if the Queen's corgi would be coming along for the adventure. Lupo felt his heart lift a little at the mention of her name. It had been a few weeks since he had seen his friend at Buckingham Palace. He put his paw in George's hand. "I don't think so. Holly is busy taking care of your great grandmother, the Queen, and keeping an eye on Vulcan!"

George wasn't ready to settle down to bed. He rolled on to his side and looked into Lupo's eyes and *whispered*, "Bad VULDUN!"

Feeling tired, Lupo lay down beside the prince and yawned. "I think it's safe to say that Vulcan won't rest until he's got his hands on the throne. That dorgi is nothing but trouble."

George nodded and stroked Lupo's soft black fur. Then he asked a series of questions in their secret language. "Do you think there are really ghosts at the Tower of London? Are there such things as animal ghosts? Is Herbert going to help you? Will Kitty? What about the ravens at the Tower – one of them stole my sandwich once when I was visiting. I don't think they are very friendly. Maybe they're involved?" George was clearly too excited to sleep.

Lupo's mind whirled. He hadn't considered the ravens. The prince had helped already. Growling softly, he answered, "Enough questions for one night. If I'm going on an adventure and you are going to help me here – we'd both better get some sleep."

The two friends snuggled up together and before

the Duchess could say "Goodnight" they both were fast asleep.

Not so far away, in the darkest part of the River Thames, a long-forgotten creature snapped its jaws in satisfaction. It began to chuckle, and this became a deep, belly-tumbling, evil laugh. Tonight had gone exactly to plan.

It was done. For too long he had hidden in the sewers, living in London's shadow. Soon the entire world would know about him. Soon he would finally have his revenge.

His black eyes studied England's finest jewels littered all about him. Humans loved their trinkets so they would surely miss these. He ran his claws over the finery and felt a lust for power growing like an itch beneath his scales. Vulcan had better keep up his end of the deal. Edgar the raven was so far proving to be a most useful pair of eyes and ears at the Tower. Eventually, the beast under the river would have to deal with them in the same way that he'd destroyed all those do-gooder animals that had come into his domain. He flicked his great tail, as if ready to wipe them all away. His claws clattered against the sewer's brickwork. Picking up the Imperial State Crown sitting on top of a pile of crowns, he slid it on to his head, feeling the joy of its almighty power. He was now a real king.

Briefly, he thought of little Alice, the princess who had flushed him down the toilet over a hundred years ago. He never imagined that getting his revenge could feel so good.

4

A Rude Awakening

Since the early hours, the police had been keeping Buckingham Palace informed of their investigation into how a thief had got past the Tower of London's security and successfully broken into the most secure safe in the world. Her Majesty the Queen had gone back to sleep, and was snoring. Holly wasn't normally bothered by the sound but it was really *very* loud. Just as she managed to settle into the perfect spot on the floor by the fire, she heard someone walking briskly to the royal bedchamber. No doubt someone with more news on the investigation.

Monty, the oldest royal corgi, didn't move, but Willow and Candy immediately stood to attention and barked in perfect unison. "Your Majesty, wake up! There is somebody at the door."

The Queen mumbled loudly. "Sssshh."

As was procedure, Holly was given the signal by Willow. On command she leapt on to the bed and walked up to the Queen's head. The royal corgi began pawing at the bed covers. The Queen groaned. "Off the royal bed!"

The peach telephone that sat beside the bed rang. *Shrill-shrill.*

Still the Queen did not move. Willow winked twice and gave the order to Holly to commence licking sequence "alpha awake". Holly licked the side of the Queen's face.

"Enough! Down, Holly, stand down!" said the Queen as she reluctantly opened her eyes. Hearing the knocking at the door she said, "Yes, come in, I am awake."

Tommy, the smartly-dressed footman, opened the door and quietly explained that the Chief Inspector of the Metropolitan Police was on the phone.

"Yes, thank you, Tommy, good morning," the Queen said, sitting up. "We were quite upset when they told us at dawn about the robbery at the Tower of London. Let's hope the inspector has good news.

Right, we think a pot of tea would be nice." She glanced at the palace canines. "And please may we have some warm milk for the dogs." With that, the Queen sniffed the air. She looked at her corgis and said, "What on earth is that smell?"

Tommy closed the door behind him and Vulcan emerged from behind the large curtains. Holly immediately noticed the Queen's dorgi had an unusual look of amusement on his face.

The Queen got out of her large bed and wiped away her cold cream. She put on her thick glasses and her comfortable sheepskin slippers and zipped herself into her pink dressing gown before picking up the telephone.

"Inspector, tell me you have good news . . . oh . . . I see . . . how very odd . . . Yes, I understand . . ." She sat down slowly back onto the large bed. "Yes, I am sitting down." A look of horror spread across the Queen's face. "Would you repeat that, please?"

Willow and Candy moved to Her Majesty's feet, hoping to better hear what the Inspector had to say. Monty opened one eye and promptly decided to ignore everything that was happening and go back to sleep. Vulcan watched their reaction and rolled on to his back happily.

"Let me understand this, inspector. Not only has my Jewel House been emptied – all of the stones have been taken from Stonehenge? The National Gallery has been ransacked? Every Union flag has been pilfered? Nelson has been nicked off his column? The Coronation Chair has gone from Westminster Abbey . . . oh, and one *more* thing – Dippy the dinosaur has disappeared? This is an *outrage!*"

Holly had been watching it all, and was troubled. Vulcan seemed just a little bit too happy in the face of all this terrible news. She watched as a small but definite smile spread across his face. He was clearly enjoying the Queen's distress.

The Queen continued. "A gang, you say . . . Indeed . . . A master criminal – an insider . . ."

Holly's eyes stared into Vulcan's, looking for answers. She suspected he may be involved and yet he was giving away nothing if he was. She couldn't help but turn her thoughts to a conversation she had had with Lupo a few weeks ago, during his visit to Buckingham Palace with the Duchess. They had been walking around the garden when the royal spaniel had said, "Vulcan seems too quiet. Like he is plotting something. Normally, he's chasing me out of the palace but today he's nowhere in sight. That's odd. It can't be a good sign, Holly. We both know how dangerous he can be."

Holly had laughed off Lupo's concerns. "Honestly, Lupo, he's just being a bit mysterious. Besides, even if he did come up with a plan to take the throne, he'd need an army and where is he going to get one of those from?"

"If I know Vulcan, he'll find a way," Lupo had replied. She remembered, just before he'd left that day his warning: "Will you keep an extra close eye on Vulcan for the time being? If you see him behaving differently, we'll know he's surely about to get us all into something awful. Call me crazy but there is nothing good about Vulcan acting mysteriously."

Holly had long been aware of Vulcan's feelings towards Lupo. It was true the royal dorgi was obviously more than a little bit jealous of the love and affection the nation heaped on to the Duke and Duchess's spaniel. The royal dorgi sneered at the television when the spaniel was on parade. Holly remembered one afternoon when he'd paced the living room, saying, "I don't understand why that common spaniel has been given such adoration! Will someone explain to me how he's been allowed to disgrace the House of Windsor with his presence?"

Monty had dismissed his ramblings. "You sound like the old servants. Remember that story I told you when you were a pup, Vulcan – the one about Princess Alice and her royal reptile pets?"

Vulcan had cut Monty short. "It's not the same!"

Holly had seen the look of sadness on Monty's face. "You never told me about Alice," she said.

"Well then, Holly, we'll just have to go and have a nice walk around the palace and I'll tell you all about Princess Alice and her royal reptiles," Monty said with a smile.

There had been a change in the royal dorgi's behaviour since then. He'd been around less and less. Holly hadn't noticed him at breakfast, or supper for that matter. He was disappearing for long periods of time.

Still on the telephone, the Queen had started making notes. "The sewers, you say . . . escaped via the Thames, you say . . . Hmmm this really is a development. Thank you for the update. We must focus our efforts on getting it all back to where it belongs . . . of course, yes, the State Dinner . . . indeed it is tonight. Hmmm, well, then it is of the utmost importance that the criminals are caught."

The royal dogs watched as the Queen replaced the receiver and sat in silence, her hands folded across her lap. Holly was concerned. She had never seen the Queen so lost in thought. The loss of the royal crown was clearly concerning her.

"Well, dogs, I can't be without a crown! The nation needs to see that the monarchy cannot be undermined! It looks like I just might have to go and see the ghostly Lady in Blue."

Holly whispered to Willow, "Who is the Lady in Blue?"

Willow shook her head. "I think I know, only I don't think any member of the royal family has seen her for years. Naturally, there have been rumours but I have never seen anything to suggest the Lady in Blue actually exists."

Monty's loud snores distracted everyone long enough for Tommy to return with a silver-plated tea tray which he placed on the table nearest the fire, making sure that the Queen's armchair cushions were correctly puffed up to Her Majesty's liking.

Holly caught a glimmer in Vulcan's eyes. Whilst the other corgis began stretching for the busy day ahead she visited him in his corner behind the curtain.

She took a big breath in and tried to be as brave as possible. "What's going on, Vulcan? And don't you dare play the innocent. You look like you have been up to no good. I saw you sneaking in behind Tommy earlier. Where have you been? Even Lupo noticed you are not around as much as normal. What's going on?"

Vulcan turned five times to the left before tucking his short legs under his body and resting his head. It had been an especially busy night. He was in no mood to have a chat with Holly. He began to growl at her. "Leave me in peace, Holly. You have no right to watch my comings and goings. You haven't the faintest idea how important my work is. Animals are the future – and the sooner you get on board with that idea the better. Enjoy the Queen's undivided adoration," he said scornfully. "You won't have it for much longer. Now, be gone."

Holly was shaking like jelly. She was convinced

that he was in some way involved in the robberies. Frustratingly she just didn't know how. She settled herself near the fire and tried to think of a way to get a message to Lupo. She wished she had taken his warning more seriously.

At that moment, the Queen returned from her dressing room with Candy trotting alongside her. She was wearing a smart navy blue day dress and her mother's pearls. Making herself comfortable with a cup of tea and a basket of warm toast at the card table next to Holly, she rang a small gold bell. Tommy entered the room, "Yes, Your Majesty, how may I be of assistance?"

"Tommy please could you get all the dogs washed, one of them has been up to no good – I can distinctly smell it!"

5
Mucky Pups!

Holly had decided she would track down Herbert to
give him a message. The only problem was, finding a
tiny mouse in a great big palace required a skill only
Lupo possessed. Although she tried, she struggled to
master the art of "sniff". The last time she had seen
Lupo she had been impressed with his incredible
sense of smell. Trying to find Bernie was proving
harder than she'd imagined as she kept getting
distracted by a strange dead fish smell she had noticed
earlier that morning in the Queen's bedroom. She
had only just begun looking when she was scooped
up by Tommy.

"Bath time, little missy," the footman said merrily.
"Andre the groomer is ready for you at the salon."

As they walked into the Palace's private dog salon,

Holly saw Candy languishing on a soft red velvet cushion under a blow dryer whilst Andre brushed and trimmed her fur.

"She's so pretty!" Andre beamed. "Yes you are, Candy! Such a pretty, pretty corgi." Candy clearly loved Andre's attention. She turned to the other corgi. "Holly, I am thinking about *diamonds*. All this talk of jewels has got me thinking. Don't you think we royal dogs should be given some? All of those jewels locked up in a big stone safe. I'm not surprised someone stole them all – what a waste. I'd look good in diamonds, don't you think? I'm not talking about too many – just a little tiara will do. It would really suit me. Not sure about you, though. You have a big, fat head. Perhaps you would look good in some bracelets or maybe a ring or two?" The vain dog seemed unconvinced by that. "What! Don't look at me like that. I'm just saying, we could all do with a bit of jazzing up."

Holly sighed. Ignoring Candy, she looked around for Vulcan.

Andre whipped over to his assistant and said, in a French accent, "Did you hear, they took Nelson right off his perch. Whoever it was, they had to be quite the climber and no one saw a thing! Oh no! Quick, get the *angry one* out of the tub – I totally forgot him!"

At that moment, Vulcan emerged from the now-cold bath, looking like a half-drowned rat, and shook himself dry. He was clearly extremely annoyed at being forgotten. Holly resisted the urge to giggle at his misfortune.

"That's odd." Andre wrinkled his nose. "Vulcan has left a stone in the tub. Must have picked it up on his travels. How you dogs get so smelly and dirty living in a palace is beyond me. Right – time for a bit of perfume everyone!"

Holly watched as Andre threw the stone across to the bin. It missed and landed on the floor next to it, giving her a perfect opportunity to take a better look at it. It wasn't an ordinary stone. It was a diamond. A large perfectly cut but dirty diamond. Holly rubbed off the mud and watched as the light of the room was cut into a thousand shards by the pure stone. The robbery! This had to be part of the crown jewels. So Vulcan was involved, she thought, tucking the stone into her fur before anyone noticed.

Vulcan was seething at what had just happened.

That stone was for his private collection.

Willow's pointed nose twitched. "What *was* that smell, anyway?" she asked him. "It certainly wasn't me. It smelt like decaying fish in every corner of the palace! It just won't do!"

Everyone agreed that the pong was everywhere and none of the royal dogs liked fish.

"The palace mice need to work harder," chided Candy. "They're quite lazy – always late making my bed. Honestly, standards in this palace are slipping!"

But Holly was too busy watching Vulcan to listen to Candy's moaning. She looked over to the mean dorgi and watched as an evil grin spread across his thin face. Once again, her legs turned to jelly. Fear gripped her tummy and she thought, *Fish*. That's the second clue. What would Lupo do? She watched as the groomer's assistant followed Andre around. He'd follow the clues and gather evidence. All I need to do is follow the stench!

6
Snap, Cackle and Caw

Vulcan was happy to be clean after a bath. Finally out of the fluffing room, he was quick to make his way to the basement where the King of the Thames needed him. He hated having to bow down to anyone – least of all a dirty great beast – and it was the first time he had been genuinely terrified of another animal. But he'd made a mistake trying to bully the ruler of the Thames into doing things his way and had only just escaped with his life.

There was another thing. Edgar's role in the robbery didn't sit quite right with him. The raven had a separate plan and Vulcan was sure it didn't include him . . .

Edgar's rat servant Claw was late. Agitated, he tap,

tap, tapped his beak against the stone wall, vowing that if the rat came back with bad news, he'd eat the foul creature. "That rat is pushing his luck," he said out loud.

Edgar was the oldest of the Tower of London's black ravens. "Nasty" and "dastardly" were the Yeoman's pet names for him. Confined to the Tower since the day he was born, he was a martyr to his own misery.

With a long black talon, he kicked over a plate of food – white bread and a bit of old sausage – left by the raven master. Human food didn't sit well in him. He preferred to forage for his own tasty morsels. Sometime during the robbery, he had seen a small round bird trying to flee the action. He had plucked it clean out of the air just before dawn. After tearing away most of the flesh there was not much left of it. With his long sharp beak he pecked at the tiny bones until all that was left were some feathers and an eye that hung loose, staring up at him, and dangling by a thin red-purple vein.

Nervously, Edgar's black eyes darted around the room. He disliked being watched by anything – dead or alive. Using his long black wing, he flicked what

44

was left of the creature into his pile of carrion.

Just then, the Tower's bells began to ring. The tourists flooded in past the police cars and officers all guarding the busy crime scene. Once the visitors realised that there was nothing to see they turned their attention to the raven keepers, all eager to meet the Tower's famous raven residents.

Someone was calling his name. It was Jonas, no doubt. Hopping on to the old fortress wall just outside his cell, Edgar spied the young yeoman dressed in a cape, entertaining and educating the captivated crowds. Two of the younger ravens were doing tricks – they skirted the bottom of the cape, hanging on, showing off their skills in exchange for treats.

"Creeps," Edgar sneered, sickened by the raven's cheap performing antics.

"Why don't they fly away?" a visitor from China asked as he merrily snapped pictures.

"Oh, no," Jonas answered. "They're too well-fed for that – too fat!"

Everyone laughed.

Edgar cawed. "Soon the humans will all pay for their insolence!" Scanning the scene, he caught sight of a couple from India and their young daughter.

The girl wore a pale pink ribbon at the end of her perfect black plait. He wanted the ribbon! As the girl drank from a fountain, he jumped on to her shoulder and snatched it away. His prize in his beak, the raven jumped back into his cell. "Too fat to fly? Huh!" he said, as he flapped his clipped wings.

Jonas apologised to the little girl as she cried. "Please, everyone, be careful," he said with mock seriousness. "Those ravens need a bit of respect. After all, the legend says that the fate of England rests with those birds. Everyone, please, come and listen, please gather around – the day the ravens leave the Tower will be the day England falls. That's why we clip their wings so they can only fly short distances. We don't want them to leave, do we, children?"

The little girl stopped crying and smiled sweetly up at Edgar. "I'll let him keep my ribbon."

Jonas led the group away. "Keep an eye on your backpacks – we don't want scraggy old Edgar trying to escape. This way to the spot of Anne Boleyn's execution!"

Edgar tore at the pink ribbon. No one understood the torture he had to endure. Entertaining the masses made him uncomfortable. The grey skin beneath his feathers prickled uncontrollably as the other ravens began to caw, rattle and bleat.

Life at the Tower was not like it used to be. Back in the Middle Ages, the ravens used to have regular meetings, gathering in large numbers to discuss how best to protect the nation, the monarch and the city's defences. His ancestors had been proud and noble creatures. They'd flap their wings and people would dive for cover, such was the respect and fear they'd commanded. It was a sad fact that the ravens at the Tower had become but a shadow of what they once were. Today's meetings were squabbles about tourists and litter. His most loathed topic was, "How best to defend the Tower from chewing gum." He chortled with disgust.

From his cell, he watched the other ravens as they performed for the over-excited visitors. He ignored the cries for his attention. An evil anger had developed over the years and now it ran right through the centre of his cold, dark heart. "Look at those pathetic, useless birds. I can't stand it!" he said, pacing back and forth.

He slumped into the darkness of his cell, comforted only by his piles of bones and rubbish. His thoughts turned to the robbery. It looked like everything had gone according to plan. He double-checked himself, making sure he hadn't missed anything. He couldn't risk upsetting the new King – he needed the King to think that he was in charge. He gulped hard and wiggled his neck around, happy that his head was still on the top of it. One slip-up and the beast would end his life.

A long queue of tourists plodded away from the security barriers, disappointed to have missed the wonder and spectacle of the missing jewels. Edgar leered at them. "Oh, so sad . . . come all this way and there is nothing left for you to see . . . HA!"

It started to rain and he sank back a bit further into the grey stone walls of his cell. Just then, the small wooden door opened, and Claw stepped in. Dead bird feathers whirled around in the air. Dodging them, the rat walked forward. His step, Edgar noticed, was unusually decisive. "YOU'RE LATE!" Edgar chided.

"It's done!" Claw said proudly, thrusting out his paws, eager for his reward. "They have everything."

Edgar swept the falling feathers out of his path with a wing. He debated whether to have Claw as a ratburger but then decided since there was good news it would have to wait for another day. Ignoring

Claw, he toyed with a small feather. He could still hear the bird's screams – and savoured the delicious moment, then pulled himself back and refocused.

"The police are everywhere, searching for clues, Sir," said Claw, tugging on his long whiskers. "You have left them all baffled! Might I offer you my humble respects. Your plan worked! England is all in a muddle!"

"Why, that *is* really good news. Thank you, Claw. What's happening at the Jewel House?"

"Not much. They seem to be putting lots of yellow cones around everything. There are loads of police."

"Everything is gone?"

"Yes, exactly as you intended."

Edgar cawed loudly. "Most excellent indeed! And what of the Coronation Chair from Westminster Abbey. Where is that precious object?"

"The King has it," said Claw. "In fact, he was sitting in it as I left. I even watched him eating a bowl of fresh tadpoles with the Coronation Spoon. He really *is* a king now, isn't he?"

Edgar hopped over to Claw. "He's a real king today but he'd better not get too used to that chair or the crown jewels!"

"You must be very pleased with me for helping you," said Claw, holding out his paw once again, but Edgar didn't respond. "I think the King's army will try to take back the Tower tonight." Claw held out the other paw but again was ignored.

Edgar's eyes glittered. "Success is all mine!" he cackled. "I am brilliant. Totally brilliant! Claw, you can only dream of being as brainy as me. England will soon recoil at its own arrogance and complacency. No longer will she take me for granted!"

He added, "Yes, Claw, you have done well."

Claw eagerly anticipated his much-deserved prize, but he was also cautious. "I'm not sure how we're going to get rid of all those reptiles once they are here. Tower life just won't be the same. I doubt the tourists will come and visit with them beasties about."

"Claw, come now – trust in Edgar," said the raven. "I shall not fail. For you," he said. Claw looked down at the bird's eye in his paws, then over to Edgar who stood in the middle of his cell as if on stage, fat with his own importance.

"For a job well done."

7
The Black Route

News crews were gathering in large numbers along the outer stone walls of the Tower of London. The story had spread like wildfire throughout the world. Everyone was keen to discover who and why someone had stolen England's national treasures. The Duke and Duchess sat watching a red-faced, red-haired royal correspondent on the news explaining the significance of the loss to the nation.

Lupo watched his family's disappointment growing by the minute, then set off to meet Herbert. The spaniel was able to pick up the mouse's scent mixed with something else all the way down the hallway. The strange smell drifted right through their Royal Highnesses' bedroom and into the large dressing room beyond it. "Herbert, you smell awful!

Will you please get out of my mistress's dressing room?" he said, coughing and spluttering at the stench.

The Head of MI5 stepped out from between a white dress and a coat, leaving a distinct mouse shape on both. He was covered from head to toe in some kind of slime. "Lupo," he said, "it's worse than I could have imagined it. I'm sorry about the smell. It was the only way I could escape. I had to dive into a barrel of dead sewer fish."

Lupo sniffed the little brown mouse then sneezed in revulsion.

"Apologies," said Herbert, "it's most unpleasant, I know, and only old tea bags and lemon juice can get rid of it. I've tried chilli vinegar in the past but that leaves a rather red rash and it's incredibly itchy."

Lupo was interested in only one part of Herbert's explanation. "Did you say, escape?"

"Sorry, yes, a momentary distraction," said Herbert. "I received a report that said that there were strange animal footprints at each of the crime scenes. The police at the Tower also found something very interesting. I've been to investigate and, Lupo, you were right! I don't think this is just a matter for the humans after all. I went to the Tower via the old sewer system that runs alongside the City of Creatures and found this!" The little mouse produced a pristine ruby. "It's from the royal collection – of that I am sure. The tunnels down there are so narrow that only an animal could have used them. One other thing, Lupo. I could have sworn *something* was watching me, though I never saw it. I was covered in mousebumps. It was terribly scary. *Something* tried to grab at me. I didn't see what it was, I just ran – I ran all the way here. You must come with me right away. Lupo, this may be our only chance of finding out who did this!" The brown mouse was quite out of puff by the end of his explanation. But he found the breath to add: "There is one smallish problem – we'll have to go down the Black route. I'm afraid it's the only way to get you to the Tower without being seen."

"But both you and Kitty said it was dangerous," said Lupo.

Herbert nodded. "Yes, we did. In any other circumstance I would stand by my own advice but today is different. The whole of London is one giant crime scene. The place is crawling with police. We're just going to have to take great care and hope that whatever is lurking in the shadows stays there!"

Lupo knew he had to go. "If it's the only way then that's what we must do."

Herbert danced from one smart hanger to another and slid down a checked coat until he landed next to some black high heels. "Believe me, I wish there was another way. If you could fit through the grates I could take you via the sewers?"

Lupo sniffed the mouse. "If I'd come out smelling like you, I'd rather take the Black route, thanks."

Herbert wiped his glasses. "Quite. Well, let's get started. I presume Kitty is staying here?" Lupo nodded, so Herbert continued. "Fine – it's just the two mouseketeers today then!" he said, chuckling to himself. Lupo wasn't laughing. "Right then . . . Well, there are a few rules if we're going down that particular route. Number one: stick together. Don't leave my side. Two: whatever you do, don't look behind you. Three if anything touches you. RUN. OK? Got it?"

Seeing the look of horror in Lupo's eyes, the Head of MI5 sounded quite stern. "The entrance to the Black route is at the back of the cupboard – it's this way."

Lupo could hear George and his sister's little feet upstairs in the playroom. They were probably playing soldiers and maidens again with Nanny. He wanted to go and join them, only he knew that this was the perfect opportunity for him to slip away unnoticed. Reluctantly, he followed Herbert through to the darkest corner of the dressing room, where he could already feel a cold draught. He didn't want to admit it but he felt ill-prepared for the adventure that lay ahead.

"There's one other reason why I can't take you in via the sewers," Herbert said. "They're completely blocked, because they're chock-full of dead fish. Someone has gone to a lot of trouble to prepare enough food for a small army. The sewers under the Tower are being used as some kind of food storage."

"Food for an army?" queried Lupo. "Herbert, we need to find out *whose* army." Herbert nodded slowly. Lupo mused. "Interesting – we have a master thief and an army who feasts on sewer fish. The two have to be linked."

"Exactly, my friend. Someone is planning something big and it's up to us to find out exactly what! I suspect the jewels were just the start of something much bigger," declared a worried Herbert. "And we need to stop them."

The Black route wasn't nearly as smart as the Red route, which led all the way to Buckingham Palace. In fact, the Red route was luxury compared to this passageway, where thick cobwebs hung from the ceiling and the floor was covered in insects. To Lupo it smelt musky, like the inside of an unloved cupboard. As he and Herbert made their way deep beneath Kensington Palace, Lupo couldn't help but notice the pictures on the walls. On the Blue and Red routes, the pictures were of celebrated royal animals. Creatures of all kinds adorned the walls in elegant and sometimes dainty frames. Down here there were only dusty and very old portraits of animals looking far from happy. Lupo felt himself shudder. "Who are they all?" he finally asked Herbert.

"We tried looking into some of their stories," answered Herbert, trying to sound as matter of fact as possible. "Mostly they were prisoners, but others were given to the ruling king or queen of the time. Keep an eye out for the pictures of really scared-looking animals – we think those are the ghosts of some creatures who came down to the

tunnel and were never seen again."

Lupo stopped walking. He felt a cold chill behind him. Then something moved in the shadows. His tail stopped wagging instantly. "What was that?"

Herbert spoke in a whisper. "Rule Number Two: remember to keep walking and whatever you do, don't turn around!"

Lupo longed for the simple comforts of the other routes, such as lights lit by sparrows and soft carpet managed by mice. His paws rubbed the floor hoping to feel something familiar. In the dimly lit passageway, he could see that the carpet was threadbare and damp, unloved and worn out. The palace mice had neglected this route. When a bat flew overhead, Lupo leapt clean out of his skin in fright.

"It's only a bat – they aren't so bad," Herbert reassured him. "We use them to monitor things down here. They're spooky but incredibly useful for surveillance."

Herbert looked back to Lupo and saw something gliding though the empty darkness behind them. It wasn't a bat! He squinted through his glasses. To his horror, he saw that they were being followed. A dark shadow of an ancient beast with long, sharp claws rasped and reached out with thin, scaly arms, narrowly missing Lupo's tail. "Just don't look behind you – and try to remember rule Number Three!" With that, the mouse began to run.

Lupo was baffled. "Wait up! Why shouldn't I look behind me? What is it? Herbert, slow down! I can't keep up!"

Herbert had looked at the plans for the route the day before so he knew that there were three good emergency exit routes should they need them. The first was coming up. It was a thick steel door to the left, with a wide wheel on its front. "See the wheel?" said Herbert, as he ran. "All we have to do is turn it and we're out of here."

"I can see it!" answered Lupo, relieved that he'd soon be out of the Black route.

They made it to the door. Herbert leapt on to the wheel. A drop of liquid hit the floor.

"Is that water?" asked Lupo, as another droplet landed on his back.

"Yes, it's dripping through the door, that's all," replied Herbert, frantically racing to turn the wheel. Round and round he ran – there was little time to waste. When he dared look back, he saw pairs of eyes staring and, worse, closing in on them.

Lupo was feeling less confident and in one foolish move he turned to see what was behind him. "GHOSTS!" he barked, racing to Herbert's side. "And they don't look very happy."

The two animals began desperately turning the wheel together, frantically trying to escape the ghosts who were staring at Lupo with envy. Their decaying faces loomed out of the darkness and their brittle paws, hooves and claws grabbed at the air as they pressed forwards, trying to reach out and trap Lupo and Herbert in their cold, icy grip.

Eventually the wheel began its final rotation and just as the door clicked open, there was one more surprise for Lupo. Water started flooding into the Black route. The ghosts began drifting away as if they knew what was about to come bursting through the door.

"You see, we're right under the Thames. This is the first chamber – we need to swim in and open the other hatch, which should take us up into the Tower. You can swim, right, Lupo?" Herbert asked at the last possible moment.

Before Lupo had a chance to reply, the exit was

open and the river's cold water gushed in. They pushed through the door and shut it behind them. Within minutes, they were up to their necks. Lupo had to swim against a forceful current that kept pushing him down. He kicked hard but was barely able to keep his nose out of the fast-moving water.

Something quick and slimy swished past his left paw. He dared not attempt to think about what it may have been. All he could do was fight to stay alive in the dark water. Feeling lost and alone as the waters covered his head, he took in one great breath and dived beneath. He had to blink several times to let his brown eyes focus. The tiny mouse was directly ahead and looked like he was swimming towards a narrow doorway and what looked like another hatch.

Lupo followed Herbert though the second hatch – it was easy for the mouse since Herbert was a good swimmer. His long tail whipped against the current and he glided through the water. Lupo had to work much harder. His heavy paws punched the water and his long ears kept getting caught up in the churn and covering his eyes. It was like wearing a black mask. Lupo liked to swim but this was not his idea of fun – not like being in the bath playing bubble crown with Prince George. He was battling icy cold water and the way out was a narrow tunnel. He needed air badly and it felt like a very long time before they squeezed down the tunnel and Herbert pointed upwards. They just about managed to surface before he'd completely run out of air.

Lupo looked about for something to grab on to. There was what appeared to be an old wooden pier up ahead. With a few more kicks, they made it and both began trying to clamber out of the water. It wasn't easy. Lupo's entire body felt shattered from the mighty underwater swim. He barely had the strength to heave his body on to the old pier as they both stood in silence, trying to catch their breath. A sign above them read: *TO THE DUNGEONS*

Herbert was the first to speak, ringing out his green cardigan.

"Well, here we are. Lupo, welcome to the Tower of London!"

8
Beyond the Boundary

Lupo had been beyond the palace boundary plenty of times before without being detected as missing. However, on this occasion, his absence from the nursery was noticed by Prince George. The toddler prince didn't like that his baby sister was taking all his favourite toys and throwing them around the room. When wombat was tossed behind the bed, George followed it. It was then that he discovered that Lupo wasn't under it. Grabbing his wombat, he called out, "Lupo?" But the royal dog did not come.

George ran up to Nanny, who was knitting in the bay window and asked, "Nanny, where's Lupo gone?"

Nanny and the Duke and Duchess began searching high and low. They ran up and down the main staircase and in and out of different rooms.

The Duke even crawled under the dining room table. The Duchess ducked behind the big sofa and Nanny looked in every corner of the nursery. But Lupo was nowhere to be found.

When they'd finished searching Apartment 1A, they moved on to Apartment 2 and found Kitty curled up in George's uncle's bed, luxuriating in the middle of a mid-morning doze.

The Duchess picked Kitty up and asked, "Kitty, have you seen Lupo? He was here this morning but no one has seen him for quite some time. We are all hunting high and low. George is terribly upset."

The Duke walked in to see his wife speaking to Kitty. "Darling, why are you talking to the cat? It's not as though she understands you." Then, muttering to himself, as he searched under the bed for Lupo, he said, "Honestly, I can't understand why everyone makes such a fuss of that cat. It arrives on the back of a milk float, gets adopted by Kensington Palace and now lives in my brother's bed!"

"I know, I just thought that maybe she might be able to help us," replied the Duchess hopefully. The Duke said something about checking with the front gate security and disappeared.

"Kitty, I think Lupo is in trouble," said the Duchess. "Perhaps you'll have better luck trying to find him." The Duchess put Kitty down on the floor and stroked her tabby fur. Her large blue ring sparkled in the sunlit room. Kitty meowed as the Duchess left.

Kitty sprang into action the very minute the door was shut. "I knew that pampered pup would do something stupid that would end up getting me into trouble! Grrr. All I asked for was a few days off! Yet again, it is up to me to save him. Honestly, when I get my hands on that dog . . ."

A bottle of champagne in the corner of the room rolled across the floor. Inside were two drunk mice called Grace and Uma. They had terribly sore heads when Kitty forced them out of the bottle.

"OUCH!" squeaked the mice.

"I need you two to take me to MI5," said Kitty.

Uma and Grace looked at each other, stunned, and promptly burst into hysterics. "As if we could take a CAT to MI5! That is the funniest thing we've ever heard." Grace was doubled up on the floor, clutching her sides. "Can you imagine it, excuse me, everyone – we've brought a cat to see you

65

all! That's priceless!"

Kitty was less amused. "NOW!" The tabby had never been to MI5 before. Of course she knew where it was but had never dared to go so near to the Peter Pan statue in the middle of Hyde Park.

They popped out next to the statue and not far from the Serpentine Lake. A little girl was feeding the ducks with her mother. She turned and saw Kitty with the two mice. Kitty tried to hide but it was no use – the little girl was frantically pointing. Fortunately, her mother was too busy throwing bits of old bread at the ducks to notice Grace and Uma rubbing two bronze mice on the bottom of the statue.

Kitty heard the statue click. The little girl's jaw dropped open in shock as she and Kitty watched the entire statue twist and curl open. Grace and Uma gave each other a high five.

"It's down there," the mice said.

Kitty winked at the little girl, who waved back. Looking inside, Kitty saw that she could just about manage to squeeze in. Once they were all in, the statue closed behind them. An aroma of mice filled her nostrils. She breathed it in, enjoying the intoxicating scent. "Heavenly," she meowed to herself.

The HQ of MI5 was a world like none other. It was, in fact, a cat's idea of paradise. There were mice everywhere of all different sizes and colours. They all seemed to be extremely busy. Kitty could see one group examining a monitor, which displayed all the missing treasures now missing. Another group were testing what looked like diamonds that had been found near the River Thames. The team nearest Kitty seemed captivated by a police radio, which was reporting on the crime scene at the Tower of London.

"4–1 THIS IS 3–2. SIR. WE HAVE FOOTPRINTS. MUDDY FOOTPRINTS. OVER."

"3–2. THIS IS 4–1. WHAT KIND OF FOOTPRINTS? OVER."

"4–1. THIS IS 3–3. WELL. SIR. I THINK THAT THEY COULD BE CROCODILE FOOTPRINTS. OVER."

"3–3. THIS IS 4–1. CROCODILE FOOTPRINTS? ARE YOU SERIOUS? OVER."

"4–1. THIS IS 3–2. 3–3 NEVER LIES, SIR. IF

HE SAYS THAT THEY ARE CROCODILE FOOTPRINTS THEN THEY ARE! OVER."

In fact, the mice were so busy, none of them seemed to notice the palace cat standing in the middle of their underground offices. Time for things to get a little bit interesting, thought Kitty. "Excuse me!" she said, loudly.

All the mice stopped and instantly turned towards the palace tabby standing in the middle of their HQ. The entire place erupted into chaos. The emergency alarm was sounded. Mice leapt and ran, and bounced and squeaked in horror.

Kitty was mildly amused at the mayhem she had caused. "STOP!" she cried. "I am not here to eat you. I come in peace," she said, bowing low, trying to show the mice how respectful she could be. The mice continued to run madly around. "Fine. If you don't stop running around I will be forced to chase you."

Every mouse stopped moving and stood as still as they could. No one dared move for fear of being eaten.

"My furry and oh so delicious friends," Kitty began. "I need your help. Lupo is missing and I have to speak with Herbert."

A brave junior agent called Pete stepped forwards and began, in a shaking voice, "You should not be here. You don't belong. This isn't a place for cats. You must leave."

Kitty bent down so that her nose was practically touching the pointed nose of the young agent. "I mean you no harm," she said slowly and in a calm voice. "But I must speak with Herbert. It is very important."

A round and red-faced white mouse stepped forwards. "He's not here. He's with Lupo. They've gone to the Tower of London."

A strange but inspired idea occurred to Kitty. "I see. So who is handling things in Herbert's absence?"

A podgy young mouse wearing a pink knitted jumper with the words I SAY BOO TO CATS on the front put up her hand. "I am his Number 2. My name is Chloe."

Kitty went on the charm offensive. "What a long nose you have! *Hmmm* . . . and what a lovely jumper. Well, then, Number 2, you and I are going to be spending a bit of time together. I want to see everything you have on this robbery so far. Lupo and Herbert have no doubt gone to investigate and together we are all going to do our best to make sure the royal dog gets back to the palace in one piece. Do you understand me?"

A tiny field mouse ran up to Kitty and whispered into her ear. Kitty listened for a moment and then spoke. "According to this mouse, Lupo and Herbert have just travelled along the Black route. We all know how dangerous that is. They could be in terrible danger. I want a show of paws. How many of you have been to the Tower of London?"

Three healthy-looking agents stepped forward and spoke in unison. "We have. We are the SAS Division. We only handle the really tricky missions. How may we be of assistance?"

"SAS? What does that stand for?" Kitty asked, bemused.

"Seriously Awesome Samuels, ma'am," replied one of the SAS mice.

"Why Samuels?" asked Kitty.

"Because we are all called Samuel, ma'am."

The two other Samuels looked at each other, a bit confused.

"I thought it meant speed, aggression, surprise," said one of the Samuels to another.

"Yeah I thought it meant surfers against sewage?" said the last Samuel.

"Enough! You three – get to the Tower and find out what Lupo and Herbert are up to. The rest of you start compiling a report on everything you have found out so far. Every mouse needs to be looking for clues above and below ground. Those jewels are somewhere and I know Lupo well enough to know that when he says that he senses something is wrong – it normally is!"

The mice conferred in little groups and then, one by one, stepped forward to offer their help because all of them knew that the palace cat was right. England would not fall into the wrong paws on their watch.

9
Chaos Rules

The Duke had looked everywhere for Lupo by the time the footman rang to tell him that his car was ready. He was needed at Buckingham Palace.

"Darling, I can't find him. I have to head over to the palace now. They need me," he said, kissing his children goodbye.

"Where's Lupo gone, Mummy?" asked Prince George, pulling at the hem of his mother's dress.

The Duchess smiled at her son. "I think he's having a terribly big adventure. He'll be back soon. Why don't we make him a banner for his return? Come on, Nanny, you go and find the paper and I'll get the paints out."

Lupo wasn't having a good day. He was wet and

covered in the green slime that coated the old Tower's walls.

"That wasn't so bad, was it?" said Herbert, looking around for something to wipe clean his spectacles.

"Where are we?" asked Lupo, looking at the heavy stones all around them. They were standing in some kind of chamber. There was little light but the stones looked old and worn by the water that had filled the room for many years.

"I can't be sure," Herbert answered. "I confess I have never actually been into the Tower this way before. I think it must be the Prisoners' Entrance. It's where the convicted humans would have been brought in by boat and dropped off. There are other exits but we needed to get out of the Black route in a hurry. The route's main way out is right under the Jewel House. By now, though, it will be crawling with humans and frankly, they are skittish enough today without seeing a mouse in a pair of spectacles and the royal family's dog roaming around."

Lupo agreed.

"We just don't want to go that way," Herbert continued. He pointed to another door. "If we turn the wheel on that door we'll find ourselves drifting away from London. Nothing more dangerous than the River Thames."

"Dangerous?" asked Lupo.

"Yes. Oh, I know you may doubt me but I warn you, Lupo." Herbert shuddered. "I have seen what swims in those murky waters and survives far below it. That river bed is littered with London's secrets."

The little mouse's obvious fear intrigued Lupo. He had never seen his friend so shaken. "Herbert, why are you scared of the river?"

Herbert wiped his spectacles on a corner of his little green cardigan and sat down on a broken bit of stone near a rotting wooden door. A droplet of water fell off the end of his whisker as he looked forlornly up at the brave dog. "I was never as fearless as you, Lupo. I was once quite lost and very afraid. You see I was one of the 'forgotten.'" Herbert smiled meekly. "My family came to London on a Royal Mail barge. We came all the way up the river from the countryside. My mother longed to be in the big city and my father promised her that once I was born he would move us to a new home. 'A bright new beginning,' he told her. Only it didn't quite turn out that way. On the night we arrived in London, it rained so badly that the river flooded and the mail barge was sunk. My father and mother clung on to me as tightly as they could but the water kept coming and eventually they let me go. I drifted down the Thames inside a bottle. All alone."

Lupo was deeply saddened. "Herbert, that's awful. I'm so sorry. What happened to you?"

"The river is full of creatures. Some you know about, fish and the like. But there are other things in that river and they are nearly never seen. I can tell you, Lupo. In that bottle I saw them all!"

"Like what? What did you see?" Lupo panted in excitement.

"So many wondrous animals! They swim undisturbed by the humans. It was incredible! The murky waters hid them well. I saw great sea creatures lost in time. Their fins were so big they swooshed the water high into the air! There were mermaids and fish laughing and playing amongst sunken ships. There's a world down there still left to discover . . . only I never got the chance."

"What happened?" asked Lupo.

"My bottle was captured. The last thing I remember seeing was a set of teeth. Long, spiky sharp teeth and scales! When I woke up I was in some kind of sewer under the river. Lupo, I was surrounded by monsters. All wanting a piece of me! A fearsome ginormous crocodile ruled them."

Lupo's eyes searched Herbert's for answers. "A crocodile?"

"Yes. No ordinary crocodile, either. I think it may have been one of Princess Alice's."

Lupo asked, "Are you telling me that there is a giant crocodile in the Thames?!" He quickly pulled his tail out of the black water.

"Yes," said Herbert, "and I'm not the only one who knows about him. I overheard Monty, one quiet afternoon in the Queen's private study, telling Vulcan all about the lost kingdom beneath the Thames. The naughty puppy had scared me off so it fell to Monty to complete the royal dogs' basic training. I was keeping an eye on things from the bookshelf. Monty told Vulcan that there was once a princess called Alice who loved to collect reptiles. Only she was wasn't so good at taking care of them. All manner of snakes, lizards and even a rare and old crocodile were allowed to stumble out of their cages and into trouble at the Palace.

"Then, one awful day, all of her reptiles went missing. The palace staff hunted high and low, only they were never found. The little princess wept big wet tears with a giant inky black spider on her shoulder. You see, Inky was the only pet she had left, because – as it turned out – Princess Alice had decided to give all her lizards, snakes and even the crocodile a bath. Since the princess knew that her Nanny would not approve of them being washed in the royal bathtub, the princess had decided to wash them in the toilet. It was a dreadfully stupid thing to do, because she accidentally flushed the toilet and they were all washed into the Thames. Like I said, I think the crocodile I saw could very well be one of Alice's reptiles."

Lupo was intrigued. "And what did Vulcan make of the story?"

"Vulcan liked it very much. I heard Monty repeating it to him at least four or even five times," replied Herbert.

"How did you escape the crocodile?" asked Lupo.

"The very same flood waters that took me away from my parents rescued me. The monsters were trying to build some kind of nest. As they were building, one of the creatures broke through a sewer wall by accident. Water flooded in and I ran out of my bottle and swam as hard as I could, following the sewers all the way to the City of Creatures beneath Buckingham Palace. I made it out by the skin of my teeth."

"And you think that crocodile is still down there?" asked Lupo, shaking out the last of the water from his large black ears.

Herbert shrugged. "I don't know. I have a small division of mice who occasionally get the odd report of strange disturbances in the water but nothing to confirm if the crocodile is still alive. Either way, Lupo, you won't be catching me turning that wheel – not for all the cheese in Cheshire!" Pointing to the slimy wooden door, he said, "I might be mistaken but I think that way should take us up to the entrance to the White Tower. Once we are up the Jewel House is just a short hop away. Keep your eyes peeled for humans. Like I said, I doubt they would be happy to see us. You ready?"

"As ready as I'll ever be – though this place gives me the chills," said Lupo, with a sneeze.

10
Nero

Holly was able to follow what remained of Vulcan's trail – it wasn't easy, though. The housekeepers at Buckingham Palace took pride in their work. Every inch of the royal residence was cleaned twice a day. Grand displays of fresh flowers were arranged every Tuesday and Thursday. As a result the palace normally smelt pristine. But even though the palace was spick and span, Holly could smell Vulcan's fishy scent. She was determined to find out where Vulcan had been.

Still clutching the diamond, Holly carefully trod through the corridors of power, sniffing every centimetre of carpet and checking behind each door for clues. She ran along the red-carpeted main hallway all the way to the King's Study. Sniffing the carpets, she picked up the faintest trace of Lupo, but it was an old scent from when he had last visited. Her mind drifted momentarily as she thought of her friend. Once he learned of Vulcan's treachery he would know exactly how to confront the bad dorgi. Leaving the study, she headed down the back staircases to the palace kitchens. "I've checked everywhere! *How* did Vulcan get in and out?" she cried in frustration.

"Just where are you off to in such a hurry?" asked Bernie, a very presentable mouse with a neatly-chopped haircut. He was Buckingham Palace's new Head of House, a title held in much regard amongst the other palace mice. He'd recently moved from Kensington Palace and was finding his new home much better, especially since Kitty wasn't around to torment him.

"Morning, Bernie. I'm afraid Vulcan might be at it again. I could have sworn I smelt fish on him this morning. I think he must have had something to do with the robbery at the Tower. You know how much he longs to be the Animal King of England," said Holly with concern.

The mouse look surprised. "I also wondered where all that stinky sewer fish smell was coming from. Isn't that a coincidence? I'm on my way to HQ – I've been summoned. Herbert has sent word. He's after my entry and exit logs. He wants to know what Vulcan has been up to. Funny thing is Vulcan's been coming and going at all hours down that nasty Black route." Bernie looked unsure. "Mark my words, it's a terribly scary place. You won't catch any of us working down there. No, no – not for all the cheese—"

Holly was thrilled that she now knew how Vulcan had been getting in and out. "Bernie, please can you get word to Lupo at Kensington. He needs to know that Vulcan may be involved in the robbery and that he's been using the Black route."

"Oh well, that might be tricky," said Bernie. "You see, Lupo's missing. The whole of KP is upside down looking for him."

Holly smiled. "Clever dog. Bernie, I bet he's already at the Tower investigating the clues. Please can you direct me to the Black route?"

Bernie pointed to the basement. "It's down there – but Holly didn't you hear me, it's no place for a royal corgi."

"I'll be fine. I need to help Lupo," she said,

running in the direction of the basement staircase. "Bye, Bernie and thanks!"

It took Holly a while to get down to the basement. She had to dodge several security cameras and half a dozen bustling palace servants. Sure enough, just as she neared the route's entrance, she picked up an overwhelming stench. "Vulcan, you were here, weren't you? I can smell it!" she said with satisfaction.

The dust had recently been disturbed, but Vulcan had clearly attempted to brush away his footprints. Bravely, Holly pushed against the brickwork at the back of an old blackened fireplace and found that the Black route's entrance opened easily. The ground was wet, as if water had recently passed through it. In the darkness, Holly felt cold and lonely. Little wonder the happy palace mice avoided the route, it felt like a very sad place.

Holly took her first steps inside. It was quiet, apart from the sound of dripping water coming from further down the passageway. The constant *drip drip drip* happily distracted her from her fear. Holly looked at the pictures Lupo had seen earlier with similar sadness.

"Poor things. Look at the state of this place. No

wonder no one wants to come down here. It's all so drab and lonely."

Something moved and – out of the corner of her eye – Holly was sure she saw a pale spirit. When she turned her head to get a better look, it was gone but she had the distinct feeling she was being watched. "I know you're there," she said. "Why don't you come on out and introduce yourself? I'm not here to harm anyone."

A slow-moving mist gathered around her. With interest, she ran her paw through it. "How curious." The mist then took various animal forms. The largest was a lion. Holly was shocked. "You're *ghosts*! I never saw animal ghosts before!"

The ghosts crowded around her. Biting her lip she resisted the urge to bark in terror.

"Why aren't you barking?" asked the softly spoken lion.

Holly remained calm. "Well, I know that you are not going to harm me, are you?" she said tentatively.

The Lion panted. "Harm you? Why would we want to harm you? Just because we are ghosts doesn't mean we want to hurt you."

Holly was surprised. "That's good. Then why are

you following me?"

"This is a very dangerous place," answered a small Pekinese next to the lion. "There are monsters down here and if they catch you . . . well . . . you'll end up like us . . . lost for ever."

The lion stepped forwards and bowed his head. "It's an honour to meet you. I am Nero and I am the guardian of the lost animals."

Holly bowed. "I'm Holly. It's a pleasure to make your acquaintance." She looked around at the gathering of exotic creatures, all watching her with interest. "How did you all get here?"

Nero spoke. "Some of us came from far away lands as gifts for great kings and queens. Others came here and were captured and locked up. We became the Tower's ghosts once we died. We protect the Black route. It is by our service that we pay our dues."

A Pekinese pushed her way forwards and nudged at the lion's large paws. Nero said, "This is Annabel."

The nervous dog sniffed Holly. "Like me, you are a royal dog."

"I don't understand – you were a royal dog?" asked Holly.

Annabel tiptoed back and forwards. "Oh yes.

I belonged to Queen Victoria. One day I came down here to explore and the next minute I was captured."

This was all news to Holly. "You were locked up in the Tower?"

Annabel shook with terror. "Yes. If it weren't for Nero I never would have been found. You must return to the palace. Like Nero said, it's too dangerous for you down here. Leave while you still can."

Holly refused to leave. "I can't go – I need to find my friends."

A dainty greyhound drifted in front of her and cleared its throat, speaking in a posh voice. "The dorgi ran through here this morning. I saw him myself. He calls himself Vulcan. He's been down here quite a bit. Rude thing. You can tell him from me – we ghosts dislike being swatted away. We're ghosts, not flies! Another dog was here this morning too. He was handsome, covered in black fur. Regal, I would suggest. A pure spaniel – fine breeding. My sister tried to get his attention and pretty soon all the girls down here were following him! Mighty handsome chap. Slipped away with a mouse."

"I see. Thank you." Holly was sure they were talking about Lupo. "I don't suppose the mouse was wearing a green cardigan?"

"As a matter of fact, yes, he was!" said Annabel.

The greyhound indicated to the left of the tunnel. "The spaniel and the mouse left by the hatch that leads to the dungeons."

Nero floated into her path. Holly looked up at the great lion's mane and into his misty grey eyes. "Nero, will you help me find them?"

Annabel barked a series of short, very sharp barks and Nero nodded.

Holly said, "I'm not afraid. Nor am I Vulcan. I am here to help. I want to get the jewels back and to find my friends."

The lion moved closer to Holly and looked into her eyes. His imposing stare made her shiver. "The robbery is our greatest shame. We failed to stop them. For this reason I will help you."

Holly felt reassured by the great lion. "Thank you."

Annabel began to shake again. "Nero, I am afraid. Please take her home," she pleaded.

Holly was comforting. "I can't leave without my friends, Annabel. I'm sorry. Besides, we have to help Lupo and Herbert find out who was responsible for the robberies last night."

The greyhound spoke. "It was busy last night. We didn't see much action down here. Whoever stole the jewels didn't use this route to get out. They must have escaped via the River Thames."

Holly was baffled. Vulcan couldn't swim and detested water. If that was the only way the jewels could have got out, it was unlikely that Vulcan had been alone. Her heart fell. She thought for a moment and then asked, "The Tower's ravens – they must have seen something?"

Nero shook his mane. "Thor and Odin saw nothing, but they aren't so bright. They flee whenever they see us ghosts. Edgar would be the one to ask. He keeps himself to himself – he's the oldest raven here. He's not the nicest of birds. But I can take you to see him."

Annabel's teeth were chattering with fear. "I think the last time that bird was happy was when he got to peck away at those human heads they used to put on those sharp stakes," she said.

Holly grimaced. The Tower of London used to be a dreadfully scary place. She followed closely behind Nero, hoping that she'd soon catch up with her friends. Nagging questions remained unanswered at the back of her mind. If Vulcan didn't steal all the jewels, what was he doing at the Tower of London? And what of Lupo and Herbert? Were they safe? Perhaps the most important question of all: who was the mysterious thief at the Tower of London? And where were all the missing jewels?

Nero pointed to an entrance at the far end of the route. "We'll need to navigate around the Tower. It's the only way to avoid you being captured – the creatures down here are always hunting for fresh meat."

11
Duck and Cover

While Holly was navigating her way to the Tower, Lupo and Herbert were entering the damp, empty dungeons at the Tower of London.

Lupo felt the cold silence scratching away at his bones. Everywhere he looked he saw headless ghosts. Herbert ignored them and tried to hurry the royal spaniel on. Lupo's tail slid between his legs in fear.

"No time for ogling," said the little mouse. "And never mind that lot. They're long gone. They hang around to try and scare the visitors – that's all. Hurry along now, Lupo. This way!"

Lupo lowered his eyes so as not to stare and caught sight of something on the floor. Whatever it was glinted between cobbled stones. "Herbert, hang on. There's something here."

"Well done, Lupo." Herbert bounced over and picked up a large, shiny green jewel. "That's an emerald and a very rare one at that. This must have come from the Jewel House!"

Lupo sniffed the brilliant green stone. "Our thief must have been in a pretty big hurry to have managed to leave it behind."

Herbert examined it and then absentmindedly tucked it into his pocket. He raced along the cracks in the floor, looking for anything else that may have been dropped. By the time they reached the staircase that led up to the White Tower, they'd found several small diamonds and one gold ring.

Herbert tucked them into a pouch he had folded up in his pocket. "Evidence bags," he explained to Lupo. "Basic mouse intelligence training: never be without evidence bags. If we head up that staircase, it should bring us out on to the courtyard. Then it's just a short dash to the Jewel House." The little brown mouse climbed up on to Lupo's ear and gripped his collar as they went up the staircase. They got to the top and Lupo let Herbert climb back down. Herbert insisted they wait. They both slid behind a large wooden door. "Basic Training Module Two – listen before reacting."

Lupo poked his head around the door to see if he could see anything. "Enough rules already!" Two police officers were heading for the door and the staircase down to the dungeons. "Quick, hide, they are coming this way."

The two of them dived into a fire bucket, thankfully in the nick of time. The policemen walked past, failing to notice the royal dog's tail poking out. Lupo jumped out after they had passed. He walked up to a larger set of double doors that led to the courtyard. Peeking through the keyhole, he could see several officers dressed in their finest uniforms. "Exactly how are we meant to get past that lot?" he asked Herbert, who was busy counting the number of strides to the door. "There are at least thirty of them out there. We will never get past them without being spotted."

"Fascinating, must make a note for the file – 102 strides to the door. That's at least six fewer than estimated. Oh don't worry about them. I have a plan." Lupo furrowed his brow, but Herbert looked confident. "Leave it to me," he said. "This is a game well suited to the Tower of London. I like to call it 'duck and cover'."

Herbert was small enough to run out of the door and through the group of officers without anyone noticing. Lupo watched him duck through to the centre of the throng of policemen and over towards the furthest corner of the courtyard. To Lupo's amazement, the tiny mouse grabbed a large yellow police cone. He raced as fast as he could back to Lupo, ducking every now and then to avoid suspicion. Lupo was astonished – none of the humans saw a thing! Herbert was out of breath when at last he made it back to Lupo.

"That was incredible, Herbert," he said. "Now what?"

"Now we cover. Climb under the cone and listen to me – whenever I say *duck* just sit really still. When I say *run* move as fast as you can."

Lupo obeyed and climbed under the cone. His long, feathered tail stuck out and was wagging merrily at all of the excitement. Herbert grabbed it and stilled it, then promptly pushed it under the cone. "And whatever you do, don't let them see you. Keep that tail under control and tucked in!"

Lupo agreed but before they could go anywhere, he proclaimed, "Er . . . Herbert, I can't see a thing under here. How exactly am I going to know which way to go?"

Herbert giggled. "Haven't you played blind dog walking before? Surely you must have played it with the children in the nursery?"

Lupo blinked underneath the cone. "I think you mean blind man's bluff. Of course, I have played it with the children but this is different. I might actually get caught and thrown into the Tower!"

"Come, come, Lupo, trust me. I know what I'm doing. It's simple, really. All you have to do is listen to me and I will guide you. And avoid getting caught."

Lupo cocked his head to one side. "All right, I trust you, but Herbert – this isn't a game where we all end up on the floor laughing."

Herbert was too busy waiting for the perfect moment. "Herbert?" Lupo began, fearing that he'd been abandoned.

"RUN!" screamed Herbert.

Lupo did as he was told. He made sure his tail was tucked in and ran as fast as he could in a straight line, hoping he wouldn't bump into anything. He looked down and all he could see were the cobbled courtyard stones beneath his paws. He tried hard to see through the bright yellow plastic of the police cone around him but it was no good. All he could see were shadows.

"DUCK!" shouted Herbert at the yellow cone speeding towards the ring of officers.

Lupo promptly sat down and did not move. Outside the cone he overheard two policemen talking. ". . . Used some kind of skin – that's what they said. Could have been a snake. But if you ask me it's one of the strangest crime scenes I have ever seen."

"Snakeskin bags? Must have been the biggest snake in the history of the world! That skin must be at least nineteen metres long!"

"RUN!" he heard Herbert shout again.

Lupo ran forwards only to collide with another cone. CRASH!

Her Majesty's Chief Inspector was the first to notice something odd. "Can someone please move all these unnecessary cones? I think the general public are fully aware that there is an ongoing investigation. There are enough of us here and if not the helicopters, news crews and missing crown jewels should warn them to avoid the area!"

Herbert ran to a cone, believing that Lupo was inside. As he climbed under he found – to his horror – there was no sign of the royal spaniel. He had chosen the wrong cone. Now he had no idea where Lupo was. All of a sudden, the cones were being lifted and moved. Herbert strained to listen for a reaction to any of the officers seeing the Duke and Duchess's royal dog.

"Got them, sir! We'll put them in the Jewel House, out of the way."

Lupo was gripping on to the inside of his cone, trying his best not to fall out. When at last the emergency cone was put down inside the Jewel House, he let go. The policemen left and he heard the door clicking shut. He was relieved that Herbert's game of duck and cover was well and truly over.

Herbert crawled out from beneath his cone. "Lupo? You there?"

"Only just!" answered the royal dog. "Phew, that was close. Too close, Herbert."

"I thought I'd lost you for a moment," said Herbert. "Glad to see you are quite well. Argh, it wasn't that bad, was it?" Seeing the look in Lupo's eyes he decided it best not to dwell on their journey to the Jewel House. "I got us here, didn't I? Might not have been the easiest of journeys but at least we are here now and . . ."

Lupo sniffed the air and immediately noticed the distinct smell of fish.

Herbert ran ahead to check that they were alone. "All clear – but I am warning you, Lupo, when I checked it out this morning even I was shocked. It's a pretty big mess."

The royal spaniel was used to big messes. After all, he spent all of his afternoons in the nursery with the children. But nothing could have prepared him for the sight that lay ahead of him. The Jewel House was arranged along several long corridors. Smart wooden cabinets that had once contained jewels now lay empty. The delicately handmade cushions upon which the wealth of England had rested were torn to shreds, as if massive claws had ripped right through them. The spotlights inside the cabinets, which ordinarily shone on the precious crowns, swords and jewellery, now only highlighted the emptiness of the nation's great loss.

Lupo and Herbert fell silent. There was nothing but destruction to witness. Not a single item from the famous collection remained.

Eventually, Lupo spoke. Lifting up a sharp grey tooth from the floor, he said, "Herbert, this wasn't done by a human. Look what I found." He held the tooth up. "Her Majesty doesn't have any crowns made of teeth. I am sure of that."

Together, they examined the tooth.

"Distinctly reptilian," concluded Herbert. "Carnivorous variety – can tell by the sharpness. I'd say by the size and weight of this thing, it's a whopper. Possibly gigantic."

"Any idea which reptile?" asked Lupo.

Herbert shook his head. "I can't be sure until we get it back to the lab at HQ for analysis." He put it into the pocket of his cardigan to keep it safe. "Our second clue," he said, tapping the side of the pocket.

Herbert suggested that they try the next corridor. Lying on the floor against the red carpet was

a snakeskin, hastily sewn together to make a huge, long bag.

"That's one seriously large snake," said Lupo.

Herbert climbed inside it and examined the pattern on the skin. It was damp. "This is a water-based snake. An anaconda, no less. More commonly found in the Amazon. This skin was shed weeks ago. I'd suggest our thief used these skins to help get everything out."

"Brings new meaning to the word 'swag bag,'" replied Lupo, investigating the strange skin.

Herbert took a cutting of the skin and put it in his other pocket. Then he went in search of more clues.

Lupo stood back and assessed the destruction. "Herbert, this couldn't have been the work of just one thief. This was a carefully organised crime. Someone on the inside must have known the value of the jewels and that the Queen would be lost without them. Also, there's no evidence that someone broke in. See – the main door is completely intact. That means that they had to have the keys!"

Herbert picked up a black feather from the floor. "A raven's feather, Lupo!"

At that moment, Lupo heard footsteps coming towards the room they were in. "Quick, someone's coming!" he said. But they were too late.

"What do we have here?" said the Chief Inspector.

"A dog," replied one of the policemen.

"I can see that! Get him. I won't have a dog running loose in my crime scene!"

12
Caught in the Act

After being chased through the Jewel House by several policemen, Lupo was cornered. He had no choice but to surrender. With Herbert missing, he sat down and waited for the officers to grab him.

"Come on, it's a dog! Someone grab it!" the Chief Inspector ordered.

Lupo bowed his head, as a mark of great respect.

"Lock it in the Tower. Then someone call the Mayhew Animal Home. Make sure you tie him up good and proper."

Lupo had hoped none of the officers had noticed the royal tag on his collar. But as a lead was attached to it, one of the officers said, "Hang on, sir, we have a problem. This isn't just any stray dog. This is Lupo."

"*Who?*" questioned the Chief Inspector.

"He's a royal dog and he belongs to the Duke and Duchess, sir."

Edgar was watching as the royal spaniel was escorted out of the Jewel House by three policemen. "Look who it is, Claw? It's Lupo, come to visit my Tower!" he said proudly.

Claw bounced over and peered out from beneath his master's wing. "What's he doing here?"

"I don't know, Claw – go and find out. He's not part of my plan and I'd hate him to get in the way."

Claw scurried out of the cell and Edgar watched as the buck rat quickly caught up with the police. A young officer was helping a group of lost tourists find their way out of the Tower since the Jewel House was closed. Edgar watched as he put his police radio on to a bench next to where Anne Boleyn had lost her head. In one quick hop, he was out of his cell and across the courtyard. Neither the officer nor the tourists saw him swipe the precious radio.

"I'll be taking this, thank you, officer," he

squawked as he hopped away with the radio in his talons.

Nanny and the children had only just returned from the park – the Duchess had wanted to see if Lupo was out chasing squirrels. The telephone rang in the kitchen. Nanny was giving Charlotte a cuddle when she lifted the receiver. "Hello, this is Kensington Palace. How may I be of assistance?" she said politely.

Princess Charlotte *gurgled* – she liked the noisy telephone. Her teddy bear fell to the floor. The Duchess scooped down low to pick it up.

"Oh . . . oh my, yes I will inform their Royal Highnesses immediately." With that, Nanny hung up the phone. Princess Charlotte waved her arms in the air. Her nappy needed changing. Nanny was shocked. She turned to the Duchess and said, "That was the police. Lupo has been found."

"Finally, that's really good news. Where is he?" questioned the Duchess.

"Well that's just it, ma'am. He's at the Tower of London!" answered Nanny.

Princess Charlotte was delighted. Dribble bubbled

from her big smile. Prince George ran to his mother's side and pulled at the corner of her jumper. "DODO!"

The Duchess put her hands on her hips. "How on earth did Lupo get all the way to the Tower of London?" Nanny shrugged. Hurriedly, the Duchess pulled her coat back on. "Well, I had better go and pick him up."

Nanny smiled. "That dog never fails to surprise me."

Prince George was determined to go with his mother. Lupo was his best friend, after all. "Mummy, Lottie and I want to come with you," he pleaded.

The Duchess looked at her children and then at the clock. "Looks like we're all going to the Tower, then. You too, Nanny. If we hurry we'll be back in time for tea."

Herbert had been hiding. He watched as Lupo was put on a police lead and led towards the café. This was not good. He had only just managed to leap off Lupo's neck before he was captured. He picked up the heavy evidence bag and re-tied it to his back. He decided the best thing to do was to try and free Lupo.

"Chief said to lock him up in the Tower. So why

are we going to the café?" said one of the officers to the other.

"I fancy a cup of tea, don't you? Come on – he's a royal dog. These things have the best manners in the world. I mean, how much trouble can he be?"

Herbert could see that the officers were tying the royal dog to a chair outside. As he made his way stealthily towards the chair he bumped right into the SAS mice from Mice Intelligence Section 5. Herbert greeted them with glee. "Samuels, I have never been so happy to see you!"

The three SAS Samuels were equally pleased to see Herbert. "Sir, we have been looking for you everywhere. You have to come back to HQ. Kitty has taken over and . . ."

The little mouse's large ears flapped. "Did I just hear you right? Did you just tell me Kitty is in our HQ?"

Samuel No. 1 nodded.

Samuel No. 2 nodded.

And Samuel No. 3 shook his head. "It's pretty bad, Dude."

"This will not do at all," said Herbert. "Never mind that now. Hopefully she won't wreck the place or worse eat anyone before I get back. I need you three to create a distraction for me while I free Lupo."

The mighty Samuels all nodded in agreement. "Leave it to us," they said in unison.

Samuel No. 3 added, "Dude, we've got disastrous distractions down!"

Being small was an advantage. Herbert watched as the three SAS mice were able to dash around all the people now gathered outside the café, watching the royal dog being tied up.

"Over here!" shouted one Samuel.

"Under there!" yelled another Samuel.

"Watch me fly!" said Samuel No. 3.

The three mice were now in the café on standby, waiting for his signal.

Meanwhile, Lupo tried not to panic. His heart was thumping. Getting caught was not part of the plan. Crowds gathered around him. Tourists began taking his picture. He had no idea how to escape without causing a scene. He'd heard the policeman talking to Kensington Palace and worse than that, he had overheard that the Duchess was on her way to collect him.

By now a large group of people were all around the famous spaniel. Lupo was letting them take his picture and giving out his paw-autographs.

Herbert saw an old lady with a walking stick sit down at a table in the middle of the café with a large slice of carrot cake, a cup of tea and a marzipan mouse. He gave his signal to the three Samuels. "GO, GO, GO."

Lupo heard a loud scream. Then another. Several ladies who had just got off their coach, in need of a nice afternoon tea, found themselves under attack in the Tower's cafe. They came running out, clutching each other, waving their umbrellas and handbags around, screaming: "Mice! The place is infested! I saw them! They were flying through the air and running everywhere! One even landed in my tea!"

Lupo looked into the café. It was a scene of incredible chaos. Food was flying through the air, cups and saucers smashed to the floor. The café's waitresses ran with brooms and dustpans trying to catch three little white mice as they artfully terrified all the humans. He felt a tug and then something small jumped on his back.

"It's me. Herbert!" Lupo saw his friend grinning from ear to ear.

"RUN!" cried the brave mouse.

They wasted no time racing through the mob of unhappy tourists and policemen. Herbert spotted a narrow gap in between the old stone walls which was large enough for them squeeze though. At the same moment he jumped through he heard a police whistle and someone shouting, "*Get that dog.*"

As they raced through the gap and away, Lupo hoped that this adventure wouldn't be his last.

13
Traitors' Gate

Kitty was finding the mouse headquarters cramped, although it was thrilling to have all the mice scurrying around at her beck and call. There was nothing that they didn't see, hear or know. There were several teams now on fact-finding missions at all the other crime scenes. Reports were coming in every hour. The team at the National Gallery had found paw prints from a small dog. The theory was that a snake had taken Nelson from his column.

"Any news on the stones from Stonehenge yet?" Kitty meowed across the operations hub of MI5.

A keen young agent bounced forwards, wearing a headset, "Yes, more footprints and a development. A rat – possibly a buck rat."

Kitty licked her jaws in satisfaction. "Good, good.

This is great. You see, it's not so bad having me around, is it? Can someone get me a pint of milk and something to eat, please? All of this work is making me hungry." The mice that were around her suddenly darted for cover. Kitty smiled to herself, mischief making was such fun. "It's all right, I'm not that hungry."

Seven mice gathered around her, thinking that it was safer to report into her in packs. Kitty got up and made her way to Herbert's office. The pack followed with their reports.

"Kitty, we believe we have found Dippy the dinosaur," said one of the mice in the pack.

"Finally, some good news. Where was he?" asked Kitty, inspecting a laboratory full of mice all working on spy gadgets and repairing all manner of surveillance machines.

"He was in the sewer, ma'am. It looks like the thief used the networks of sewers around the City of Creatures to come and go with everything."

"Well, that explains how they got away unseen by the humans," answered Kitty.

The mice continued. "There is more. We found a few kittens with Dippy. It seems they have turned him into some kind of ride. They have been using his head as a boat and his tail as a slide, ma'am."

"*Tut–tut.* Kittens today have no respect!" exclaimed Kitty.

The mice had to run to keep up with palace cat as she headed for the "brain laboratory."

"We think that Dippy was too big so – well, he got stuck, ma'am," said another mouse in the pack.

Kitty picked up a mobile phone that had been turned into a car by a mouse. "Incredible," she said under her breath. "No wonder Herbert is so quick at getting around." The mouse that had been working on the phone groaned, angry at being disturbed.

"That's good – see that Dippy is freed," ordered Kitty.

The mice saluted their temporary leader. "Already arranged, ma'am. We're going to try taking him back via the London Underground. But if that doesn't work we'll have to steal a double decker bus."

"Does anyone have any update on the jewels? Or Lupo and Herbert's whereabouts?" asked Kitty, as she flicked through a basic mouse training manual.

"YES, SIR!" an intelligence mouse called from in front of a big monitor. "SAS have just reported in and they are at the Tower. They have seen Herbert and Lupo. All safe and well."

"See, it's easy with me in charge," said Kitty. "I think we are talking permanent fixture, guys. How about it? Me and Herbert? Huh?"

The team of mice around Kitty looked unimpressed and more than a little bit uncomfortable. The intelligence mouse began waving again from the monitor.

"Yes, what is it?" asked Kitty.

"The jewels. I think I have figured out why someone would want them."

"AND?" demanded Kitty.

"Erm . . ." The mouse hastily bashed at his keyboard. He eventually stood up, holding a slim bit of paper. "My report says that whoever wears the Imperial State Crown is the ruler of the nation. So I guess the thief intends to rule over us, you see?"

Kitty grabbed the page from the mouse and read it over and over again. "Not good. The Queen needs a crown. Everyone – get to work to find that thief!"

* * *

It annoyed Vulcan that Holly had dared to cross him. He had big plans that might have included her one day, but after her questions this morning and then her disappearance – with *his* diamond – this afternoon, he decided she was not to be trusted. He alone would rule. She would never understand what he was trying to do or how important his work was. The age of the animal was now and he was ready to stake his claim to the throne of England. Just knowing that the Coronation Chair and the Imperial State Crown were safely tucked away, ready for his big day, made him feel powerful. He puffed out his white chest and practised his kingly walk.

The Queen was, of course, distressed but he knew that she too, in time, would come to appreciate the need for this small change. Of course the royal family would be allowed to remain at their respective palaces after his rule commenced but their jobs would need to be addressed. There would be no place for any human who wasn't prepared to bow down to him or respect the small alterations he had in mind.

Vulcan ignored Tommy the footman, who was

whistling, and trotted past the corgis, who were deep in conversation, pondering the reason why anyone would want to steal all the union flags along the Mall. Vulcan's top lip curled. Taking all the flags had been *his* idea. Once they saw his designs for the new flag they would understand.

The grandfather clock in the yellow living room ticked loudly. It was time he got back to check that everything was ready for the next part of the plan. He had a few minutes to look in on the Queen to see what was being said in the meeting and taking place in the main living room.

The Prime Minister was sitting a little too comfortably on the yellow sofa nearest the monarch, in Vulcan's spot. Vulcan growled lowly, trying to imagine what job he would give the Prime Minister once he was on the throne.

"Your Majesty, it has left us all deeply concerned about what might be coming next," said the Prime Minister. "We have found various animal footprints and tracks. This could be the work of an organisation we have yet to gather intelligence on – or worse – this could be the start of some kind of zoological invasion! I hardly think this is the time for a state event.

We can't have the world's leaders here. Honestly, I think we have to think about rescheduling tonight's state dinner," concluded the Prime Minister, standing abruptly.

Candy batted her long eyelashes at the man in his smart blue suit. She liked the way his cheeks flushed when he was talking to the Queen.

The Prime Minister paced around the room like a bulldog that had been caged up for too long. Vulcan quickly hopped on to the silk sofa and resumed his spot.

The Queen stroked Willow, who was sitting comfortably on the royal lap. "We will do nothing of the sort, Prime Minister. The event will proceed as planned and we will make sure that the culprits behind this mess are brought to justice to pay for their treacherous crimes!"

The Prime Minster stopped pacing and returned to the sofa as the Queen took a call. He clicked his fingers at Vulcan. "Move, dog, move. These are important matters of state. OFF!"

Vulcan stared villainously up at the man in his turquoise tie.

"OFF, MUTT!" shooed the Prime Minister.

Vulcan snarled. He had no choice but to get off. As he hopped down on to the smart plush carpet, he muttered under his breath, "CAT LOVER. When I rule his new job will be as an official pooper scooper!"

It was time for phase two of the master plan.

Holly had made it into the raven's lair. She found herself standing in the middle of group of small cells. The doors were open and inside she could see Thor and Odin cowering. They were less than happy to see the lion Nero with a royal corgi in their home.

Odin's eyes swivelled round and round as he examined the unwelcome visitors. "I don't know what you are doing here. But we told you before. We didn't see anything."

"Yeah," cawed Thor. "Edgar told us that we didn't see nothing."

Odin smacked Thor over the head with a short clipped wing. "Thor, you dumb-dumb! He didn't say that. I remember: Edgar told us not to tell anyone about the keys! You are really stupid."

Holly growled, "Odin, keys?"

Odin hopped about, crashing into things in his cell. "I didn't say that! Not me! It was Thor!"

Thor was not happy about being accused. "No, it wasn't! It was Edgar who said that we shouldn't say anything to anyone about him taking the keys. Not me!"

Odin hung his head and, shaking his long beak, said, "Thor, I don't think I have ever told you how really, really, really, stupid you are."

Nero walked out of the cells and Holly followed, leaving the two ravens to squabble amongst themselves.

"So Edgar stole the keys to the Jewel House!" said Holly.

Nero nodded and then looked towards the outer wall. "Look over there. Are they your friends?"

Holly was astonished to see Lupo and Herbert diving through a gap in the wall, being chased by several policemen, some old ladies with cake all over their faces and three white mice. "Quick! We have to hurry! Where are they heading?"

"They're heading for Traitors' Gate. We might be able to stop them before it's too late."

"Traitors' Gate?" Holly was struggling. Her tiny

118

paws were dwarfed by the great lion's paws. She did her best to follow closely behind but the cobbled stones and darkened corridors seemed to go on for miles. "What happens if we don't get to them in time?" she panted.

"There's a world beneath the Thames – the entrance to it is through Traitors' Gate. If your friends enter, they might never return," replied Nero.

Holly found that all of a sudden, her paws moved faster than they had ever done before and she was shocked to find herself running side by side with a lion.

14
Beneath the River

Herbert knew that there was an old passageway hidden within Traitors' Gate – the gated entrance to the Tower of London which was half submerged under dark water.

Lupo had a bad feeling. "Why is it called that?" he asked.

"It's where the traitors were dropped off. It's disused now, but there is an archway hidden underwater. We just have to walk down the steps and swim through and find it. I'm pretty sure it's how the thief got in and out."

Lupo didn't like the look of the cold water lapping the edge of the staircase. "I'm beginning to wish someone had invented a doggy swimsuit."

Lupo took the lead and began walking down the

narrow stairs. When he got to the last step he helped Herbert climb on to his back. "You cling on to my neck, and don't let go. I'll swim straight down."

"Like I said, we are looking for an archway of some kind," said Herbert, preparing to get wet. "I don't think it's particularly large. My reports say that we need to swim through it."

"OK, are you ready, buddy?" Lupo breathed deeply.

"Ready," said Herbert, grabbing Lupo's fur.

The dark water was cold. Lupo dived down in search of the mysterious archway. When at last he saw it, both he and Herbert were almost out of breath. As they swam through the arch and up, the water began to drop. They clambered out, grateful to be able to breathe again.

"This must be it." Herbert pointed to a black wooden door. They pushed it open and found that they were at the entrance to a brick tunnel.

"That smell – it's the smell from the Jewel House," suggested Lupo.

"Sewer fish," replied Herbert.

Lupo sneezed several times. "That is disgusting. Are you telling me that there are fish that live in the sewers?"

Herbert's whiskers twitched. "Yes. They aren't pleasant either. But they are a source of food. They live off . . ."

Unimpressed, Lupo interrupted, waving a paw in front of Herbert's face. "No need for an explanation, I get the picture. Yuck! Gross!"

It wasn't too dark in the tunnel but it was cold, and it didn't help that the two friends were soaking wet. As they shook themselves off, Herbert began scurrying around. Mice can't stand being cold. Lupo smiled as he watched the Head of Mice Intelligence leaping around uncontrollably, trying to get warm.

His smiles were short-lived. Something came out of the darkness. In a flash it had them both in its claws. Lupo struggled but the more he tried to break free the stronger the creature held on. Lupo couldn't see it – or Herbert. Just a set of dirty pointed teeth.

Herbert shouted: "It's got the pouch, Lupo! It's after the jewels."

Something terribly old and twisted answered the little mouse's squeaks. "You two thieves are just in time for dinner."

* * *

Holly had seen Lupo and Herbert slipping under the water, but was too late to stop them.

"Where are they going?" she asked the lion.

"They're going to meet the King of the Thames." The lion started to walk away, his head hanging low as if he had been here many times before. Holly reached out and grabbed Nero's large paw. The lion looked towards Traitors' Gate and said, "If you follow them, be very careful, dear Holly. Many animals have gone down there and never returned."

Holly stared pleadingly into the lion's eyes. "I have to try and save my friends." The lion remained perfectly still. Holly let his go of his paw. "Thank you," she said. "Thank you for helping me."

As the lion began to walk away, he roared loudly back at her. "If you need us, you only have to call. Good luck to you, Holly. May you and your friends be safe and well."

Bracing herself, Holly braved the freezing waters. It took some time to find the entrance to the hidden royal passage. As she pushed open the wooden door, she reminded herself to tread carefully, heeding the lion's warning. She was afraid.

Holly had only just come through the door when she witnessed Lupo and Herbert being bundled into a sack by a monster that looked like a cross between a crocodile and a lizard. She called out: "LUPO!" and the monster turned around. She dived behind a pile of rocks in the nick of time. "You have be clever, Holly, be brave," she told herself and stifled her cries. "The only way you are going to save them is if you aren't caught too!"

The monster couldn't see anything, so started to move away. Holly waited until it was safe for her to follow without being seen. She kept her distance as she followed the strange monster in silence, watching her every paw tread, smudging them away so as not to alert any other monsters to her presence.

The monster turned a corner and then walked into a giant nest. Holly gasped. "This is not good."

Holly had seen a wasps' nest once in the grounds at Highgrove. Thousands of angry insects had surrounded her as she'd tried to explore their home. Standing on the edge of this nest she realised that if she were caught, she would most likely suffer more than a few stings. This nest was festering with monsters. Hundreds of them packed into tight archways, calling to each other in gruff screams. The noise and smell was immense. In the middle of it was a clearing, where carcasses of dead fish and animals had been used to fashion cooking pots, pans, knives and forks, chairs and tables. These monsters clearly liked to eat together. A pot of bones was bubbling away. She tried not to think of what might be on tonight's menu.

As her eyes grew more accustomed to the low light, she looked around for exits, searching for a quick route away from the nest, which thronged with danger. She took refuge behind a pile of rubbish. The humans who had cast it carelessly into the Thames could never have imagined that it would end up here. If only they could see who was collecting it fathoms beneath those grey and murky waters.

A rainbow of colour caught her eye. Bottles had been stacked together to create a giant underwater window before which shadows passed. Swimming in the darkness were ginormous fish and swift mermaids with terrifying teeth. No wonder the ghostly lion had warned that the River Thames was far more frightening than she had ever dared dream.

Two monsters began arguing. They were standing

under a slim shaft of light, pulling at the sack that contained Lupo and Herbert. It was Holly's first chance to get a good look at the captors. They looked like crocodiles with snouts and spiky tails better suited to a riverbed in Africa than London, yet they walked upright. At the end of their longer arms were fiercely sharp claws. Their eyes were also bigger and had black slits that flashed under the soft light. Using their snouts they called out for their master, asking him to come and see the prisoners.

The whole city began to shake, like some terrible earthquake was coming. Holly felt her paws knocking together in pure fear. "Whatever that is, it sounds large. What terrible monster is master to this lot?" she whispered to herself.

Lupo smelt it before he saw it, and Herbert seemed genuinely scared for the first time ever.

"Come out of the sack. There is no use hiding. I want to see the little thieves," the King of the Thames spoke in a dark raspy voice.

Lupo crawled out from the sack first. To his horror he found himself in front of a huge crocodile. He began to bark, fearing the worst for himself and Herbert as the walls of the nest writhed with beasts creeping ever closer.

The crocodile snapped its jaws and hissed loudly – its tail swung back and forward as if to show off its superior strength.

Lupo's eyes darted around the nest searching for a quick escape route but there was nowhere to run. He felt fear for the first time wrapping itself around his heart as it began to beat faster and faster.

The crocodile was blue with the largest grey teeth he had ever seen. As its great jaws opened wider, Lupo saw that it was missing a tooth – the tooth from the Jewel House.

"It was *you!*" Lupo barked, as he stood on the sack trying to protect his friend from the other beasts as they lurched forwards, ready to take a bite or two.

The crocodile swung its great body around and Lupo saw the precious Crown Jewels spilling down the scraggy, scaly skin. The terrifying beast snapped its jaws closed. "There is no use trying to escape. You're dinner – FRESSSSSSHHHHH MEAT . . ." He flicked the sack with his tail, which sent Herbert flying.

Herbert swallowed hard. "Um—" He was clearly scrabbling around for the right words which eventually finally came to him. "Your Highness, we humbly beg your pardon . . . we were most unaware that . . ."

"A mouse. A tiny bite for me. Hmm, I'm hungry. I think I will eat you first," spat the crocodile, rousing the interest of the entire nest.

A large number of monsters raced out of their hiding holes – more ugly crocodiles, some slimy eels, a pair of giant snakes, overgrown spiky spiders and lizards – and crowded round, keen to get a look. Herbert trembled. The monsters enclosed them, sniggering and kicking joyously.

Lupo could see the crocodile's amusement. It leered forwards, scaring off the monsters and any others that were getting too close – claiming Lupo and Herbert for himself. Snatching up the little pouch of stolen gems, he held it up to his dark eye. "Trinkets!" he said. Then, in a more menacing tone, "Get the big pot out. TONIGHT we feast. Tomorrow we shall take back the palace and I will have my revenge!"

Lupo couldn't help himself. He began to growl defensively. "Those jewels are not yours. They belong to the nation and I will never let you attack

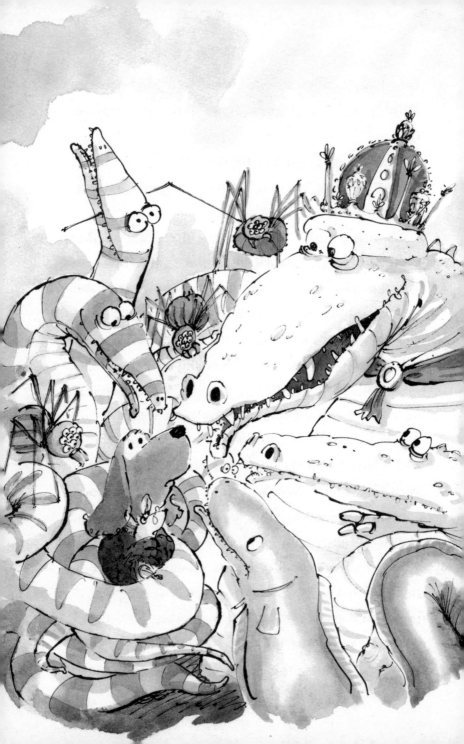

the palace."

In the fraction of a second faster than Lupo could have ever predicted, the crocodile swung his great tail, knocking Lupo to the floor. It was a smack so hard it took Lupo several minutes to find his feet again.

"You and whose army?" jeered the brute. "I AM A KING AND YOU ARE IN MY CITY NOW. I don't know where you have come from, DOG, but you would be wise to know your place. Remember your manners." He picked up Herbert and studied the tiny brown mouse. "Like your plump little friend." The Crocodile King snapped his jaws wide open, threatening to swallow Herbert whole.

Lupo barked, "STOP, please don't eat him!"

Herbert bounced high in the air out of the crocodile's stare. "WAIT, SIRE, WAIT. Please, we are unaccustomed to your ways. Before you eat us, you might like to remind us who you are . . ."

The Crocodile King's black eyes froze. Herbert tried again, knowing that they were seconds away from being consumed. "You were Princess Alice's crocodile, were you not? Oh, King of All Things Below and Beneath the Great River Thames . . . Oh great one!"

It worked. For now, Lupo watched as the Crocodile King squinted, inspecting Herbert with fresh eyes. "What do you know of Princess Alice, MOUSE?" In a flash, he leered at the crowd of creatures looking on, who withdrew almost as quickly as they arrived. "Useless creatures. Get back to work: the whole world will be watching when I take the throne!"

Holly covered her mouth as she saw the Imperial State Crown resting on a bed of bones.

The King of the Thames scooped up Lupo and Herbert and heaved his gigantic body into the air. "We have some things to discuss before dinner, you and me, MOUSE. CHOP CHOP . . . tick tock, it's nearly dinner time, DOG."

Now that the crowd had gone, Holly came out of her hiding place and walked behind the great king's pointed tail. On close inspection, the crocodile had to be over a hundred years old. It dragged its tail behind him and its enormous claws twisted and churned up the ground as he walked. The crocodile swung itself in through a door crudely marked up with the words:

KEP AUT MY ROM
King's stuff

Holly inched her nose around the door and then her head. The King disappeared deep into his private quarters.

She said, far too loudly, "The nation's treasures. It's all here!"

For now she was safe, which was more than she could say for Lupo and Herbert.

15
Dinner Time

Prince George and Princess Charlotte were sitting in the back of the car. George was trying to explain to his sister that Lupo was in trouble at the Tower of London and that it was up to the two of them to save the day.

"I'm a brave Prince, you see?" he said to his mystified sister.

"Gooo?" she replied.

"Yes, I am!" answered George. "That means that we have to . . . um . . . Dodo needs our help and that's that!" he tried to explain.

"DODO?" asked Charlotte.

"Dodo is in trouble, so when we get to the Tower you have to scream – a lot. Make sure Mummy takes you to the baby room so that I can go and find him, OK?"

The youngest member of the royal family gave a double thumbs-up. Screaming was something she did well!

Lupo heard Holly, and so did Herbert. Lupo could also smell her: Holly had the most distinctive scent, that not even the overpowering stench of the nest could mask. To Lupo, Holly smelt like freshly cut grass. He breathed in her heavenly scent and listened hard. When Holly walked it was with a slight shuffle, which made her collar rattle in a certain way. It was this noise he heard as the King dragged them into his domain. He knew he had to get out of the crocodile's grip. He couldn't let the King catch his beloved Holly.

As they arrived in the King's room, Lupo's eyes fell on a sight he wasn't prepared for. Artworks from the National Gallery and rocks from Stonehenge lay littered all about the floor. Amongst these priceless objects were the Crown Jewels. At the top of the pile was a chair, which Lupo realised, to his horror, was the Coronation Chair.

The King was revelling in his surroundings.

He pulled Lupo and Herbert closer to his huge body and said, "How did you get in here? Right under my snout, you clever little thieves."

Piled high, the collection of jewels looked like rubbish thrown together with little care for its worth. Herbert was aghast. Hundreds of years' worth of history littered the room, discarded haphazardly. On the floor next to a collection of England's kings' and queens' crowns was a large, half-empty snakeskin bag. Spilling out were the treasures that had been looted from the Jewel House.

The King of the Thames dropped Lupo and Herbert right next to it. "I will discuss your crime from my new throne!" He heaved himself towards the precious Coronation Chair.

Herbert winced, too frightened to watch, for fear that the ugly crocodile would flatten the precious chair.

Lupo sniffed the snakeskin. In barely a whisper he said, "So that's what that was! Somehow, they must have filled the skins and pulled them down here."

Herbert agreed. "It's the same anaconda skin! Look!" He pulled the cutting he had taken from the Jewel House from his pocket and, sure enough, the patterns were identical. "They aren't your normal run of the mill snakes – they are big, very big and they live in water. Let me tell you, we are in serious trouble if he has one of those things down here." Herbert hastily flicked through his mental Book of All Things. "From what I can recall, they really quite like eating mice, dogs, goats, and even humans."

The Crocodile King was watching his prisoners. "CHITTY CHATTY, I can see you two down there. Tell me, DOG – what do you know of Princess Alice?"

Several smaller alligators entered the room at this point, looking for their dinner. Lupo spied them. Clearing his throat, he said, "Your Highness, we are very impressed. This is quite a palace! Princess Alice would have been proud that you have survived all this time down here. Boy, there are so many of you now . . ."

The King rocked back and forwards in the old wooden Coronation Chair. Herbert's nerves jangled with every splinter that fell from it. The Stone of Scone, underneath the old chair, slid back and clanked loudly. Herbert winced, thinking of the precious history that was so recklessly being toyed with by the scaly monster.

"ALICE abandoned us," growled the crocodile. "She flushed us away like we meant NOTHING. I will have my revenge. I have everything I need now to rule. All that is left is to take Buckingham Palace, which I will accomplish soon. Very soon."

One of the crocodiles attempted to snatch Herbert away. The King leapt from his throne and bore down on the hapless creature. "LEAVE US. Bring me that snivelling VULCAN."

Herbert pulled on Lupo's left ear and pointed over to Admiral Nelson who was propped up in the corner – a pigeon sat stone still on his shoulder, still paralysed with fear. It was a long way from Trafalgar Square, after all.

Lupo could see the concern on Herbert's face before the mouse said, "That's NELSON. You can't just shove Nelson in a corner. Lupo, we have to get this all back to where it belongs! The minute Vulcan gets down here we shall be done for. If Vulcan tells him who you are – well, he won't hesitate to eat us!"

The King started putting on rings and necklaces from the royal collection. "GET MY CROWN!" the crocodile snorted loudly and a small, skinny, lizard-like beast raced in, carrying a twisted crown of knives and forks with some barbed wire.

The King grabbed the home-made crown and flung it across the room. "NO! Not that one. That's my old crown. I want to show the thieves my NEW crown. HURRY UP! CHOP, CHOP, or you'll be eaten with them! And tell them to make it snappy with that pot," he demanded fiercely. "Tell them to make sure it's nice and hot! I don't want these little thieves not cooking properly for my last meal down here. I want it to be extra TASTY."

The lizard returned moments later, bowing humbly. It presented the King with England's Imperial State Crown on a cushion made out of a dusty potato sack.

Lupo and Herbert exchanged keen glances. This was the closest either of them had ever been to the Queen's Imperial State Crown. Herbert had told him all about it in his history lessons. Lupo watched the precious gems twinkle in the faint light as the King put the crown on his flat head.

Once again, Herbert pulled on Lupo's ear. "We have to get that crown back." Then, spotting a missing emerald, he said, "Look, Lupo. There are meant to be eleven emeralds on the crown and I count only ten. The missing emerald must be the one we found in the dungeons," he said, patting his pocket.

Lupo studied the crown and saw that Herbert was right.

"SHINY, ISN'T IT?" said the King. "I like the purple velvet – it really sets off the colour of my eyes." The vain crocodile held up a gold plate and used it to admire his own reflection. "Don't you think it suits me?"

Herbert almost fainted. Lupo steadied him with his paw.

The lizard servant spoke but the King struggled to hear it. "What was that? Speak louder!" he bawled.

Lupo watched as the old King strained to hear. "He *can't* hear, Herbert. The King is as deaf as a post!"

Herbert was happy. "You're right. At least he can't hear any of us. That's something. Now all we have to do is come up with a plan to get out of here before he gets around to cooking us!"

Now the lizard was trying to act out what he wanted to say in an attempt to explain matters to the deaf Crocodile King. But the King was growing, frustrated. "WILL YOU STOP DANCING AROUND AND TELL ME WHAT THE MATTER IS? I WAS IN THE MIDDLE OF TALKING TO MY SUPPER."

The lizard ran over to Lupo, then back to the Imperial State Crown. Lupo knew they had somehow figured out who he was. But the King still didn't understand what the lizard was trying to explain. "GET OUT, this game is not fun any more," he roared. "Bring me fish. I fancy a starter before my main course," he blustered.

The slim creature looked quite fed up when it left but came back with a twisted shopping trolley filled to the brim with large grey fish muddy from the bottom of the Thames. The lizard was bowing and wheezing.

The King wafted the horrible sewer fish in front of Lupo and Herbert. Both of them had to resist the urge to throw up. "Got a salmon once. Don't get them regularly down here. Pesky mermaids get to them first. So I am stuck with whatever these are. EAT ONE. They aren't all that bad once you get past the pong."

Lupo heard something moving behind him. Whilst the crocodile was busy tucking into his revolting fish, he turned to see Holly smiling behind a large picture. His heart thumped in his chest. "Holly, you need to get out of here. It isn't safe," he whimpered.

Holly could smell the rotten fish from her hiding place next to Lord Nelson. "Lupo, I can't. I came in the same way you two did. This place is infested. Somehow, we have to warn the others. Vulcan's left the scent of sewer fish all over the palace. You were right – he was plotting."

The King of the Thames spoke with his mouth full. "Princess Alice flushed us away and this is where we all ended up – down here. Soon my army and I will be free to roam about the royal palaces. I WILL BE KING!"

Lupo had the beginning of a plan. "Holly, I will try to distract the King. You start trying to find a way out of here. We need to hurry. Herbert is right – once Vulcan gets here, we've had it."

By now, Lupo felt confident enough to approach the crocodile. Though it sickened him to the bottom of his stomach, he began eating the slimy grey fish the King had tossed in front of them. "Your Highness . . . it's so kind of you to feed us. Delicious." Lupo felt positively green. "Your nest is impressive, what else is down here?"

The crocodile ripped the rotten flesh off a large fish and replied, "You would be amazed at what is thrown into the Thames – the fine clay preserves everything. There's always a lot of money, which is useless until we melt it down and make pretty, shiny things with it." The crocodile pointed to his bed, which was made of coins all fused together. "That's where I first saw my new crown. On one of those coins, you see . . ." he drifted off, lovingly stoking the Imperial Crown. "We also get lots of other stuff – all good for building and extending the nest." The crocodile absentmindedly picked at a crab that was attempting to dart in a sewage fish carcass. "I run a brisk trade in plastic and wood. Once found an entire building in the clay – must have tipped right in. It was very old, the man who lived in it was still in bed when we pulled it out!" The King laughed and rattled his tail towards a skeleton propped up in the corner.

His tail swaggered from side to side as he rambled

on. "Not a day goes by without some creature trying to sell me an old wreck. I've got no use for old ships, although I am partial to a pearl, of course. Anne Boleyn's necklace has been down here far longer than me. Now, where did I put that thing . . ." He stepped up from the Coronation Chair and rummaged around in a chest of drawers which was overflowing with things found in the river.

Herbert's pulse was racing. He had barely escaped the last time he'd been down here. Since there was no flood, he knew they couldn't hope for a great rush of water. He had no idea how they would get themselves or the room full of national treasures out. He looked around nervously at Holly who was busy scouring the room for a way out too.

The ancient crocodile continued to tell his stories, unaware Holly was sniffing around.

Herbert called out to Holly, "My dear! Where are you?"

Holly peered out between two stones from Stonehenge. "Psssst! Over here. You should see all this stuff, Herbert. I think he has *everything* down here. When I say everything – I mean, EVERYTHING!"

"Holly, any luck finding a way out?" asked

Herbert, cutting to the chase. "Any hatches or archways?"

Holly shrugged. "Nothing yet. I'm still looking."

The King was distracted, throwing everything around in search of Anne Boleyn's necklace. "B – I always wondered what that meant?"

Lupo grabbed the opportunity to talk to Holly. "Holly, I'm not sure how long I'm going to be able to keep him distracted. Keep looking – I wish you hadn't come down here."

This made Holly cross. "Lupo, *someone* had to come and rescue you!"

Herbert said, "I hate to interrupt, but we need to hurry. Any minute now, that lizard is going to come back and we'll be in that pot. I don't know about you, but I am not OK with being eaten!"

The crocodile seemed to have found something else to keep him amused. "Shopping trollies – got so many of them. Wouldn't believe how many end up down here. They were mighty useful last night, let me tell you!"

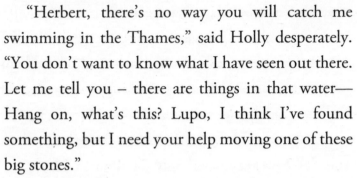

Lupo said, "I am not about to see any of us being eaten by that crocodile and his monsters."

Herbert was calculating. "We could try swimming out?"

"Herbert, there's no way you will catch me swimming in the Thames," said Holly desperately. "You don't want to know what I have seen out there. Let me tell you – there are things in that water— Hang on, what's this? Lupo, I think I've found something, but I need your help moving one of these big stones."

Herbert said, "Go help Holly. I'll keep him busy."

The crocodile clearly was enjoying the company of his supper. Herbert bounced over to him, stealing his attention. He began, "It's quite a nest, Your Highness."

"Yes, yes – it's a special place. I quite agree. I have plans, though. I think the Albert Hall would make an ideal aquarium," mused the King, rolling out a big piece of paper showing the Albert Hall filled with water. A giant squid seemed to be having a great time with an unhappy orchestra.

Herbert was horrified. "And I suppose the Tower

of London would make a perfect home for you and all your dead fish?"

"The Tower will be my fortress," explained the crocodile in a serious voice. "And it's where my wives will be. After all, a king needs heirs. I've got seventeen wives and a hundred and twenty four and a half younglings, but I *still* haven't met the perfect wife yet. A king can but dream of such things."

Herbert humphed and crossed his arms. He'd had quite enough of this cocky King. Herbert had been in love with the same mouse for years. He'd have gladly married her if only she'd noticed him.

Lupo and Holly forced the stone out of the way. She had been right. Above them was a very narrow shaft. Daylight shone down it, meaning that it led to the surface. The only problem was that it was a very narrow, long climb to the top. "Well done, Holly, this is it. We can't climb out but Herbert can."

Lupo ran back to Herbert's side just as the crocodile turned to inspect what remained of his fish starter.

The mouse started to speak: "We were wondering, Your Highness, how did you get all these jewels in here? What I mean to say is, I . . . we have such

respect for someone who could move all this treasure so quickly. Surely you must be so strong, or you have an anaconda lurking around here somewhere." He faked a laugh, hoping it might fool the King.

"You really are a clever fluffy thing! Pedro is my anaconda from South America. He swam all the way up the Thames from the jungles. Alas, he is as blind as a bat. Never managed to find a way home. He's so blind he needs a guide for most things."

"So someone else helped guide Pedro?" Herbert asked.

The King continued to spill his secrets. "Birds. Pedro only likes to use birds. So it was easy, you see. The raven was most accommodating – getting the keys for me, helping me get in and then guiding my Pedro though the narrow tunnels with all my shiny crown jewels." The King picked up his plate and moved the grey, sludgy fish around it. "WHERE IS THAT VULCAN!" he said, smashing his fist on the plate demanding attention.

16
Herbert's End

The Duchess, Nanny and the children arrived at the Tower of London to be met by a large crowd of news reporters and police, all asking how Lupo found his way to the Tower.

"Now the whole world knows Lupo is on one of his adventures!" said the Duchess as she strode through the main entrance. "Come on, everyone, let's go and get him. If that dog could talk he would have a lot of explaining to do."

Once they were in, Prince George gave the signal to his baby sister. Princess Charlotte stopped waving to the crowds of onlookers and promptly burst into tears. Nanny suggested that they take Charlotte to the baby room. "It's all the excitement," she said. "Probably got the better of her."

The Duchess agreed. "She'll be fine once we have Lupo. You go ahead, I'll take George with me."

Prince George winked at his clever sibling. He was happy to finally be on an adventure all of his own. "Now to find Lupo!" he murmured to himself.

Slowly, Herbert reached into his cardigan pockets and rummaged around for a moment before pulling out a small diary. Adjusting his horn-rimmed spectacles, he began flicking through the pages. "Easter Parade? No, that was last month. Order of the Garter – no that's long since passed and besides, it was in Windsor Castle. Prince George's birthday – no that's in a few weeks' time at Kensington Palace. HOLD ON! I think I have it. There's a state banquet planned for tonight. It says here that all the world leaders are coming to Buckingham Palace – they may be eating in the gardens – well, that's if the weather is good. The rain has been pretty bad of late but it's a nice sunny day. You don't think . . ."

Holly was convinced that was it. "Yes I do. Sounds like just the kind of event Vulcan will use to get this King into the Palace. We have to stop it. I won't have my family threatened by some stinky, leathery old beast! What's that . . . hang on that's—" She whistled from the back of the room. "Leonardo Da Vinci's cartoon is down here! I don't think Leo had this place in mind when he drew it – it's hardly the stuff of dreams . . . Wow – what is that . . . Oh no! The Queen must be pretty angry about this being taken. It's a model of HMS *Britannia*!"

While Holly was talking, the crocodile was busy mushing up the remaining first course of sewer fish with the golden Coronation Spoon. It was too much for Lupo. He bent down to Herbert and said, "He's nearly done with his first course – we are going to have to hurry. Herbert, Holly's found a way out but it's a long climb. We won't make it out. But *you* could. When I give you the signal, run."

Lupo had to think fast. He needed to give Herbert the time to climb out of the nest. For a fraction of a second, he thought of the game he would play with Prince George to delay Nanny from putting them to bed. It was a game called Kings and Queens.

"Your Highness! I would like to play a game with you. You seem like the kind of King that would like a good game of Kings and Queens."

The Crocodile King twirled the spoon around his

tongue thoughtfully, and decided a game was exactly what he needed before his main course. "KINGS and QUEENS?" he boomed. "I don't think I have ever played that game before." He stood and walked over to Lupo. "BEGIN. But be quick – the pot is almost ready, and there's tasty fresh meat for supper – you DON'T HAVE LONG, DOG!"

"Yes, let's start," said Lupo nervously. "You go and make yourself comfortable and we can get going." Glad to have the King's attention, he signalled to Holly to stand by. Then he whispered to Herbert, "COVER," and Herbert dived under a pile of union flags. Then he turned back to the crocodile. "Well, it's a fun game – you have to say which country you would most like to rule and why and how you would become king. And I have to come up with a way to stop you."

"I WILL WIN!" said the King of the Thames, drooling with pleasure.

Holly gasped. Lupo was playing a risky game trying to outwit a crocodile.

Lupo repeated the instruction. The King closed his eyes. Lupo said, "RUN!" and Herbert raced over to Holly and into the narrow shaft.

"Good luck, Herbert," said Holly as the little mouse began his long climb up.

"I am ready," said the terrible crocodile. "I am a great king. I will have America because I fancy being king of the Wild West! I will take the king of America and eat him. This is easy! Ha!" he said.

Lupo shook his head. "I win."

"No you don't," shouted the King.

"Err, yes, I do because America doesn't have a king – it has a president." Lupo's tail began to wag. He was thoroughly enjoying the game.

"Oh," said the crocodile, bemused.

Lupo pointed to Admiral Nelson. "I think I will take Lord Nelson as my prize, please?"

"Done," the King of the Thames grunted. "I never liked him anyway. I think he's a pompous grumpy lump of stone." Then he said, "MY TURN!" He turned in circles with excitement, sending piles of jewels everywhere. "I choose Switzerland because I love chocolate. I will chase the King into the mountains."

"Switzerland doesn't have a king, either. So I win again."

"No! That's rubbish. I want another turn,"

demanded the King.

"No," said Lupo. "The rules are the rules, so I will take all the stones from Stonehenge, please."

"Fine. Stupid heavy stones. Good luck trying to move them!" grumped the King.

While they carried on playing, Holly watched as Herbert climbed higher and higher. By the time Herbert was at the top, Lupo had managed to win back everything but the jewels and – perhaps most importantly – the Imperial State Crown.

"Last round," said Lupo.

"I will have England. This is easy. I will have it because I want it! Besides I already have it in my clutches."

"Oh really. And just how do you plan on replacing Her Majesty?"

The old crocodile just scratched his head and looked thoughtful . . .

Herbert crawled out of the top and was amazed to find that he was in the middle of the courtyard at the Tower of London. Luckily, the police seemed to be distracted amongst a large group of photographers. As he caught his breath, he noticed the ghost of a woman and two little boys. He immediately knew that they were the executed wife of King Henry VIII, Anne Boleyn and the princes who had been locked in the White Tower, lost for ever.

"Great, more royals. At least they're human. I'm having one heck of a day," he said to himself as they drifted towards him.

Edgar the raven watched, one eye on the Duchess and her sons; the other on the little mouse that appeared to climb out of the old drain. The radio he'd stolen earlier chattered away, telling him that the royal family was being taken to the visitors' centre. With this knowledge in mind, he chose to zoom in on the funny-looking mouse that appeared to be wearing glasses and a green cardigan. He debated for a while if he could be bothered to bounce over and capture it or if he should go and introduce himself to the royal family. He mused aloud. "Perhaps I could pick up a prince for His Highness beneath the river . . ." The funny-looking mouse would be a snack, of course, but it appeared to be quite pudgy so he decided that it could be fairly tasty.

Decision made, he puffed up his wings and switched the radio to silent and prepared himself for gliding – since flying was well and truly out of the question.

Herbert, meanwhile, was exhausted. He sat down and gave himself a minute or two to get himself together. He would need to alert HQ. He rubbed his little feet and straightened out his cardigan. Just then, Anne Boleyn floated over to him and smiled sweetly.

"Excuse me, Your Majesty," he said politely, "it's been quite a day and I really don't have the time for a chat. You see, I have to save Lupo. If I don't go and get help he's had it and I must . . ."

But before Herbert could say another word Anne Boleyn screamed. Edgar had swooped down and was clawing away at Herbert. Herbert was not about to give up without a good fight. But Edgar was so much stronger.

The ghostly Princes tried to help the tired little mouse but it was no good. Herbert lost his footing and fell to the ground. He lay on the floor, not moving.

Anne Boleyn pulled the boy princes away. "I'm sorry, boys. There is nothing more we can do. The mouse has gone."

Edgar picked up Herbert by the scruff of his green cardigan and bounded back to his cell.

17
The King's Pot

Lupo had the strangest feeling in his bones, as if lightning had struck somewhere and something awful had happened to someone he cared about. All of a sudden, he wasn't in the mood for playing games with the King of the Thames any more.

Holly looked up to the top of the shaft. She hoped that Herbert had gone for help. There was nothing more she could do except watch as Lupo tried to keep the awful crocodile distracted.

"Time's running out," Lupo said. "I'll ask the question again. You said you said you would take England – but how?"

The Crocodile King swayed under his enormous weight, his claws clattering on the side of the Coronation Chair. "My army will storm Buckingham

Palace soon enough," bragged the villainous monster. "Enough of this game. I'm hungry. GUARDS!"

Lupo looked over to Holly who was trying to follow Herbert up and out of the King's room, only she was too large. He watched as she frantically scratched away at the muddy walls of the nest, trying to create a bigger opening to climb through. All of a sudden, she stopped scratching and her pretty face turned paler. She was looking at the door to the King's room.

Lupo turned around to see Vulcan walking in. From his expression it was clear to them all that he had been down to the nest before. The Crocodile King greeted the bad royal dorgi with a simple nod. Lupo growled as the crocodile and the dorgi exchanged knowing looks.

Vulcan sneered. "Lupo . . . Well, well, well! I couldn't quite believe it when I heard that you had been captured. Holly, come out. I know you are here too."

Holly walked out, revealing herself. The Crocodile King was surprised to see another dog in his room. He leant forwards, tilting the precious chair so it creaked.

"Another dog thief in my home!" cried Vulcan. "I will *not* stand for this! Arghh, there she is! Sweet Holly – you two couldn't help yourselves, could you? You had to have a good dig around in my business. Sticking your noses where they don't belong. I can't say that I am surprised to see you here. I wondered if you might have figured out my plans when I first met the King of the Thames – all that sneaking around, months ago. But, no, you had no clue what I was planning with my new friends. We won, you lost, so I think I will leave you to die down here!"

The Crocodile King snapped at a lazy fly that was buzzing past, giving Holly a big shock.

Vulcan continued. "I warned the King that you two might get in our way. How very predictable you both are." Lupo barked angrily. Vulcan walked up to Holly and stared into her eyes, ignoring Lupo. "Where is the mouse? I know Herbert is around here somewhere."

The Crocodile King stood up and looked around the Coronation Chair. He said, "The furry little thief – he was just here." Piles of jewels slipped off his scales and fell to the floor. He was growing taller

161

and getting more annoyed. Then he bellowed loudly. "BRING THE POT! I'm ready for my main courses – and find that mouse!"

Lupo could see the fear in Holly's soft blue eyes. He wanted to run and comfort her.

"I grow weary of dogs – especially small ones and black ones," boomed the King.

Clearly, Vulcan was in no mood for the temper tantrum of a crocodile. "Calm down, your royal Highness. Soon enough everything will be ours."

"You traitor!" Holly barked at Vulcan.

The treacherous dorgi growled at Holly while he silently picked a necklace up from the floor. Holly watched the rare and priceless jewels sparkle. She could see that the bad dog was so lost in greed he had no sense of his royal position.

"Enjoy your supper," he said curtly. "Everything is ready. I have left the scent markers all over the palace. It will be easy for your army to find its way in. I would stay for dinner – because I would like nothing more than to watch the nations favourite pet get swallowed whole by you – but, alas, I have last-minute preparations at the palace."

"That's why you stank of sewer fish," growled

Holly. "You were leaving it all over the palace for the King's rotten army to find its way in!"

At this Vulcan grinned evilly. Lupo stood strong and looked Vulcan squarely in the eye, "You will fail. I will see to it!"

Vulcan walked calmly over and stopped nose to nose with Lupo. "This is the end of the line for you. The real prize is the crown and we have it. Goodbye, Lupo."

Several beasts walked into the room and took hold of Holly. Lupo ran forwards, trying to stop them. "Leave her alone!" The King swiped his long tail, knocking Lupo to the floor. Lupo struggled to stand up. "Vulcan will betray you," he tried to warn the King. "I know him! As we speak, he'll be planning a way to get that crown for himself. I don't know what kind of deal he has made with you, but he is a bad dog who means to have the throne to himself. ALONE!"

The King of the Thames bared his teeth. "ENOUGH!" he said. A large vessel was carried into the room. "Arghh! Here comes the POT."

18
Mice Eyes Only

Kitty had just about managed to squeeze herself into Herbert's office. To say it was snug was putting it mildly. Her tail roped around his desk and flicked about, searching for more room. As she thumbed through today's report of events she found her gaze landing, every now and then, on a large cabinet in the corner of the room. It drew her attention because of a sign on the front of it that read: Mice Eyes Only.

How easy it would be to have a quick peek, she thought. The words "One tiny little look, I mean, who'd know?" whispered within her. Temptation itched beneath her tabby fur, teasing her paws to reach out and take out one of the TOP SECRET files. In all her time at the palace there had been several secrets she had not been privy to, and that

bothered her. After all, the palace was her home and she felt that she rightly deserved to know as much as Herbert. Since Herbert knew everything and clearly kept extensive filing, if she could discover just a few of those little secrets she could rest more easily. "What harm would it do, I wonder ..." she purred slowly as her left paw creaked open the cabinet. Her green eyes searched the file headings.

"The Curse at Buckingham Palace, blah, blah, blah – Hampton Court, the Secret at Windsor Castle, the Labyrinth . . . Yes, yes, I know all about those . . . What's in here about Kensington Palace?" she said as her paws clawed at the tiny files. "*There* it is!"

It was a thick file, far thicker than she had imagined. Thankfully, the door to Herbert's office was closed. Taking one of his precious iced buns off a plate on the side of the desk munching away happily she opened the file and began to read:

The hidden passages beneath the palace lead

to . . .

"Boring. I know all about them," she said, tossing out pages. "NEXT!"

Maps of Animal Housing

Maps of Midnight Food Supplies

Timetables of MI5 Staff

Guards House Rota

Servants' Code Language

Lost and Found Royal Property

Princess Alice's Missing Royal Pets

The Crown Jewels and the Keeper's Lock

"That's odd. What are the Crown Jewels and the Keeper's Lock notes doing in a file all about Kensington Palace? Surely they belong in the file on the Tower of London?" She pulled out the notes and put them to one side, continuing her search for other secrets. "And what's this about Princess Alice's Missing Royal Pets?"

But before she could continue, the red office door opened and in blazed the SAS. They spun, cartwheeled and whooshed into the room so quickly that Kitty managed to slam her right paw in the cabinet as she hastily tried to shut it. "What is it?

Can't you see I'm busy?" she yelped in agony.

The three mice lined up together and all spoke at the same time. "We come with terrible news."

Kitty licked her battered paw. "What's happened?"

"Herbert has been eaten by Edgar the raven at the Tower of London," they said. "Anne Boleyn is most upset – she witnessed the whole thing, apparently. Here's her statement." They carefully put the thick pad of paper on the desk next to the top-secret file.

It was not the news Kitty wanted. She found herself fighting back tears – for not only her sore paw but also for her friend. Kitty liked Herbert, even though he was a mouse. Regaining her composure, she made a decision. "Don't tell anyone else just yet. We need everyone to keep working hard to save Lupo and Holly and to find those jewels."

Sensing her sadness, the SAS members continued. "Sorry, ma'am. We tracked Lupo and Holly to Traitors' Gate – they slipped under the water and, well, they are now gone too—"

Kitty wiped away her tears and grabbed the file she had put to one side. Unwilling to believe that she had lost all her friends in one day, she chose to fight on and continue to look for the truth. It was what

Herbert would expect of her. "Who is Edgar and why is he not in my report?" she asked.

"He's a raven – a nasty, big black bird. And that is not our report, that's one of Herbert's top secret files you are holding," they replied together.

Kitty was shocked. As she gathered herself, her eyes settled on the first lines within the file she was holding:

The Keeper's Lock is hallowed territory. It was first written about in King William's private diary. Located at Kensington Palace, it was constructed for the King's use alone. It is a set of rooms or a passageway that acts as a gateway. In recent times, it has been guarded by a mysterious ghost known as the Lady in Blue. The gateway may be used only by the ruling king or queen. No animal has ever been allowed to enter. Where it leads to or what it contains remains unknown. It is MI5's belief that it is directly connected in some way to the Jewel House and Crown Jewels at the Tower of London.

Kitty dismissed the three mice, saying that she would read their report alone.

'Warning,' she read on after the mice had left, 'The Lady in Blue may have the power to change everything as we know it.'

The warning convinced Kitty that it was her turn to act. But first she had to take a quick peek in the file about Princess Alice's missing royal pets.

Edgar dropped the mouse on to the cold, hard floor of his cell and went to turn up the police radio. The Chief of Police was barking his instruction to the officers around the palace. "*WILL SOMEONE PLEASE FIND THAT DOG!*" It was too good an opportunity to miss – he had to at least attempt to capture the Prince. "A royal child . . . hmmm . . ."

Across the courtyard, Prince George was watching his mother talking to the police. Lupo's escape had left everyone wondering where he could have gone. Prince George couldn't see his dog anywhere. He sat down on a stone step near the café. He wasn't sure how he would slip away without being seen by at least five hundred people. It was hard being a prince sometimes! Two officers offered to show him the White Tower. The Duchess agreed that it might be a nice idea.

Edgar turned up the radio so he could hear the Duchess in the background saying, "Just don't get into any trouble whilst I'm dealing with things here. If you see Lupo on your travels, tell him he's going on the naughty step the minute we get home!" Then he watched as George ran as fast as his little legs could carry him, surrounded by media and police officers into the White Tower. It was the opportunity Edgar had been waiting for. He hopped down to Odin and Thor, and said, "Tell the King of the Thames we have official ROYAL company up here!"

Herbert lay on the floor as still as he could until Edgar was gone. He'd not made a sound. He'd even managed to keep his whiskers from twitching and his ears from quivering. Although he was frightened, he had succeeded in keeping as calm as possible so that he might get out of the cell alive. Herbert was finally able to move. His plan to play dead had worked. The clumsy old raven had bitten off more than he could chew capturing this particular mouse.

Herbert poked a thumb through a big hole in his ruined cardigan. He felt weak and alone. He thought of MI5 HQ and the mice who depended on him. Then he remembered that he had left a nice iced bun in his office. He found himself hoping that Kitty hadn't made too much of a mess of the Mouse Intelligence HQ. It was these thoughts that got him up and gave him the renewed strength and determination to keep going, even though his cardigan was torn, and his pride dented after his epic battle with the raven. He felt sure that this was the same raven that the crocodile had mentioned. Perhaps this was the same bird that had been involved in the robbery? What better than a bird who could come and go as he pleased? he thought to himself. Distract the guards and steal the keys – so that the thief can enter without being noticed. Of course! Only a raven . . . a Tower of London raven.

There wasn't time to wait around to try and go another round with the menacing raven. Lupo and Holly needed him to get help. There were buck rat footprints in the cell and they were fresh, but there didn't appear to be any rat remains in the filthy, cold cell. So Herbert deduced that the rat had to be visiting or friendly with the raven. "Whoever heard of a rat and a raven being friends?" he pondered.

Touching the rat's footprints, he felt a familiar, slimy, smelly substance. "Sewer fish – the rat *and* the bird were in on the crime. That rat has been down to see the Crocodile King. So they are all in it together!"

Herbert could see that the footprints led to a small trap door at the back of the cell. As he climbed through, he found himself in a rat run that led to the City of Creatures. There was no time to waste.

19
Crocodile Nation

Prince George loved looking at the giant horses in the armoury within the White Tower. One of the Beefeaters had let him sit on one – he had even been allowed to wear one of the old helmets! He was so distracted playing with the Tower's staff and police officers that he'd completely forgotten his plan to find Lupo. The ghostly princes hovered in the corner watching and laughing as little George charmed everyone.

Meanwhile, Lupo was in a spot of bother. He was not accustomed to being tied upside down and hung directly above a boiling hot pot of stinky mush with Holly in a cage not far from him. Tonight's chef was a slithering lizard with a long purple tongue that it kept dipping in and out of the pot.

"A taste here and a taste there. I don't want to get the seasoning wrong tonight." The lizard pinned his gaze on Lupo and said, "It's been a long time since we had so much fresh meat. I can tell you, everyone is getting very excited and we just had word from Odin and Thor the ravens. A prince is looking for you!" The lizard went off in search of more salt.

"Lupo!" barked Holly nervously. "What does it mean by a prince – surely he can't mean . . ."

"GEORGE!" barked Lupo. He began thrashing around, trying to untie himself.

"Oh no. But how? You didn't tell him to come after you, did you?" asked Holly desperately. "Don't think I don't know about your secret language!" Holly raced around her cage, trying to get free.

"Of course I didn't! I don't know why he's here but that crocodile is not getting his claws into George!" Lupo strained at the ties around his paws. From where he was, he could see that Holly was locked up in a wooden cage not far from the pot. It looked like his friend would be next into the fire after him. The oily grey water spat and splattered higher and higher. "Do you think you can break out of that thing?" he asked.

"I'll give it a go," she replied, whilst sniffing for weaknesses in the cage. Does this mean you have a plan?"

"Yes. The plan is to NOT GET EATEN!" answered Lupo.

At that moment, the King and Vulcan returned to see how dinner was progressing. Next to them were the two ravens, Odin and Thor. Odin twitched nervously. He didn't want to end up in the pot. Thor stood still, awaiting his next instruction.

Vulcan watched the thick, foul-smelling fish bubble away right under Lupo. This had been more than he could have hoped for. Now, all that was left to do was to get the crocodile and his army inside Buckingham Palace. "Lupo, I'm glad that the two of you will share this moment together. It's a shame you will miss the invasion, although this time tomorrow there will be a new king and a new animal order and you will be but a memory. Farewell."

The Crocodile King was watching as the chefs got to work, stoking the fires beneath Lupo's pot.

Meanwhile, Holly pushed, shook and rattled her cage. She chewed the wood and tried to squeeze out. It was no good. The wooden prison held on to her no matter what she did to try and escape.

The King had seen enough. "COOK THEM AND THEN SHARE THE FOOD AMONGST THE ARMY. WE'LL LEAVE STRAIGHT AFTER DINNER." With that he departed, followed by Vulcan and a small troop of guards.

Lupo's ears dangled downwards so he was able to hear even better than before. The loathsome creatures were singing in anticipation of their dinner and impending invasion. "Holly, I heard something dropping when you were moving around. It sounded like a pin. Can you try jumping up and down or something. I think it may . . ."

An almighty crash sent the spluttering sewer fish pot flying from the stove – which, in turn, caught on the poles that were holding Lupo over it. In an instant, both dogs were covered from head to toe in boiling hot, cooked grey fish.

"Well done, Lupo! We're free – oh golly!" spluttered Holly. "This is beyond disgusting. Andre has just washed me. Boy, is he going to be mad about this. I stink. I stink as badly as Vulcan now. Great."

They both shook off what they could.

"Lupo, how do we get out of here?" asked Holly

in a whisper. "It won't be long before they come back. We have to hurry."

Lupo licked the side of Holly's face, happy they were OK. He bent his paw and lowered his head, "Traitors' Gate, it's the only way out." Patting her on the shoulder, he added, "And by the way I should have said it earlier – thank you for coming. If it wasn't for you we'd both be in that pot with those disgusting fish."

"Haven't you learnt yet?" she replied with a smile. "You can't have any of your big adventures without me!"

20
The Keeper's Lock

Herbert ran as fast as he could through the City of Creatures. It wasn't the easiest of routes because everyone kept stopping him, trying to get his attention. It was rare for the city's animal population to get a visit from the famous and highly-respected Head of Mice Intelligence Section 5. He ran right past their busy homes and shops, where so many of London's animals found their sanctuary and traded bits of rubbish: treasures abandoned by the humans above them and food carelessly dumped.

A pair of parrots from Green Park practically swooped him off his feet when they tried to thank him for helping extend their visit from Australia!

"Not now! I'm in the most awful hurry!" Herbert said as he dashed past. "Lupo and Holly have been captured by a crocodile under the Thames. If I don't get back to HQ I might not be able to save them in time."

"Then hop on!" said one of the friendly parrots. "We'll give you a lift."

Flying through the city, he hoped he wasn't too late and, as he passed the animal hospital, and flew high above the bakery that made his beloved iced buns, he felt terribly grateful for his life and to have got away from the raven. The parrots popped out of the City via a disused storm drain in Hyde Park. From there it was a short flight over the Serpentine Lake and on to MI5 Headquarters at the Peter Pan statue. Saying his goodbyes, Herbert entered the statue only to find that things were even worse than they were at the Tower of London.

Kitty had been and gone, leaving a list of orders and a giant mess in his office. Worse, his iced bun was half-eaten and covered in cat hair. All of his agents looked unhappy and annoyed. He decided to take the unusual step of escaping their cries of attention by jumping on to a tabletop.

"Please, everyone, listen to me. Please . . ." he

began, trying to dodge the questions now being flung in his direction.

"We need new laws. Cats can't just swan in here and take over," said one very fed-up field agent.

"Yes, sir. This simply will not do!" said an exceptionally clever mouse scientist.

"We won't stand for it," chimed a nervous security expert.

"No, I'm going on strike if it happens again. Mark my words, the union will hear about this and they won't be happy!" shouted a little mouse whom nobody recognised.

There simply wasn't time for all the mice moaning. Herbert cried, "Everyone, we are in a time of crisis. I ask you, what do we mice do when we find ourselves in such dreadful circumstances?"

None of the mice spoke. They looked at each other more than a little bit bemused. "Dunno, sir," said a plump brown farm mouse.

"Let me tell you, then. We stand together and we work together and we make it right together. That is how we are strongest, as a team. Kitty is a nuisance and I will make sure it never ever happens again, but she is also our friend and she was trying to help. Now instead of us all standing around, why don't we get back to work? Lupo and Holly are in grave danger." Another mouse was now on a table across from him waving frantically to get his attention. "Yes, you over there – why are you waving at me like a demented spider?"

"Sir, I have just received a report from the Tower of London that Lupo and Holly have been spotted. We've managed to get some bat cameras into the tunnel at Traitors' Gate. They are headed for the surface. Oh, and on a side note, the Duchess and the Prince and Princess are at the Tower."

Herbert was concerned. Things were getting tense. "Then there isn't a moment to lose."

The Chief Inspector and the Duchess were talking to the old ladies and families outside the café. Nanny and Princess Charlotte had come down from the baby room. She was bouncing around in her buggy, laughing at the sheer devastation within the café. She pointed at a gap in the wall and gurgled as loudly as possible, trying to tell her mother that Lupo must have escaped that way. To her frustration no one could understand her. Charlotte crossed her arms and humphed. At least the palace ghosts would understand her. They were her friends and she couldn't wait to tell them all about today's events.

Charlotte found herself smiling and growing more excited by the minute, for she knew that Lupo was having one very big adventure indeed.

According to the map in the file, the Keeper's Lock was a mysterious doorway between two upstairs rooms. The rooms were used as classrooms when there were visiting children. Kitty walked between the desks, staring up at the posters of kings and queens, maps of palaces and drawings of Queen Victoria. She could imagine all the children at work, being watched by their teacher and perhaps by the Lady in Blue.

The Lady in Blue was not a ghost Kitty had ever come across before, although she had heard the palace mice discussing her from time to time. The Lady was highly elusive and mysterious. The file on the Keeper's Lock contained very little information on the ghost. On page three, Kitty noted that even the palace records couldn't explain who she was or where she had come from. The tabby cat was not happy about disturbing a palace ghost, but if the ghost had the power to change things, then perhaps she could help Lupo.

She jumped on to the teacher's desk and then down to the adjoining door. Holding it open so that the door between both rooms remained ajar, she sat and waited.

Herbert was less than impressed that his 'Mice Eyes Only' files had been raided by Kitty. But he was interested to find that two particular files were missing: The Crown Jewels and the Keeper's Lock file and the file on Princess Alice's Missing Royal Reptiles.

When he had first heard about the robbery he had thought it might be possible that the Lady in Blue had played a minor role. She was the guardian of the secret passage, after all – the one that had been built exclusively for the King or Queen's use. It was by far the grandest passage within any of the palaces and had only one entrance and one exit, making it unique. Animals dared not use it. Various palace mice had tried but had ended up being chased away by the all-seeing, all-hearing Lady in Blue. Her role, it seemed, was simple. She would wait until anyone without royal blood tried to cross into the passage, then she would scare him or her away.

Herbert thought about the file as he attempted to pick off the tabby hairs left on his half-eaten iced bun. Tapping the edge of the file, he thought to himself: Kitty has gone to Kensington Palace to talk to the Lady in Blue. Which means she thinks the Lady can help us. She could be on to something – but why has she taken the file on Princess Alice? Putting the iced bun down wasn't easy but it was for the best, since he didn't relish the prospect of eating any cat hair.

Herbert immediately dispatched his SAS team to Buckingham Palace to keep an eye on the Heads of State and then went to inspect the monitors. The bat cameras in Traitors' Gate showed Lupo and Holly hiding behind a large boulder. A monstrous reptile army was trudging its way towards them.

Anxiously, Herbert looked at the two agents next to him. "Have we sent the extraction team in?" he asked. "Lupo and Holly need all the help they can get."

"They are still en route," one of the agents replied,

"but that army is getting ready to move. By our count twenty more of those monsters have gathered in the sewers beneath Buckingham Palace. There is no sign of Vulcan or the King of the Thames, sir."

Herbert anxiously regarded the stopwatch hanging from the monitors. "The state banquet begins shortly," he said. He looked to the far left screen and, sure enough, the Prime Minster and the President of the United States could be seen walking up the stone steps through the courtyard entrance at Buckingham Palace. Both men were smiling and shaking hands completely unaware that the Crocodile King and his savage army were about to attack.

Herbert fretted. "Looks like all the Heads of State are arriving right on schedule. Oh dear – that doesn't give us much time."

Kitty couldn't explain why the room felt so cold. Tentatively, she walked up to the door and examined

 it. There was no sign of a tunnel at first. It was only when she turned her head to the

side that she saw what must be an optical illusion. There was, in fact, a slim corridor between both doors with a tall trapdoor. She pushed it with her paw and heard the catch on the door release. It was wide enough for one person at a time to squeeze in. Once you were in the passageway, it widened and led to a staircase. She surmised that this staircase had to run behind the master bedroom, the nursery bathroom and kitchen walls of Apartment 1A. There was no sign of the Lady in Blue so she walked in and began descending the stairs.

The passage was light and beautifully preserved. It felt like an exquisitely crafted piece of furniture because everywhere were carved wooden statues of members of the royal family. Fine golden mirrors adorned the walls, so the light from the rooms behind her streamed in and filled the passage. As she sniffed, she could distinctly smell lavender. It was getting stronger and stronger and then there was a noise, like the sound of a thousand papers rustling. It got louder and louder until it stopped right behind Kitty.

The palace cat leapt around and saw the most beautiful woman she had ever seen dressed in a flowing blue dress and staring down at her like an unhappy teacher.

"Hello," Kitty tried. The Lady in Blue did not respond, but she did move closer to Kitty. "I'm sorry, but before you chase me out of here, please let me explain," Kitty began. "There has been a robbery at the Tower. All the crown jewels have been stolen. I am in a desperate in a hurry to save my friends. I thought you might be able to help?"

The Lady in Blue still said nothing. Instead, she bent down and looked into Kitty's eyes.

Kitty tried to be brave. "OK, I think you understand me, so if it's all right with you, I am going to follow this passage to the Tower of London and save the royal pets!"

The Lady in Blue finally spoke, but sounded vague. "Royal pets . . . hmm . . ."

"Yes, I'm very worried, you see, as I left Mice Intelligence Section 5's headquarters . . ." The Lady in Blue looked confused, so Kitty tried again. "Look, my friends have been captured by a crocodile – a big one – one that has a big army of other reptiles. They have been living under the Thames for a long time and—" Kitty stopped. The Lady in Blue had turned her back; she seemed troubled.

Kitty felt dreadful. The last thing she wanted to do was offend the mysterious ghost. "Did I say something to upset you? If I did I'm so sorry."

The Lady in Blue closed her eyes and Kitty felt wind all around her and she knew something unbelievable was about to happen.

21
Monty's Duty

Her Majesty stifled a yawn and sat on the end of her bed. Willow stood to attention next to her. Candy lay by the fire and Monty was, as usual, asleep in the stripy blue armchair nearest the door. "Willow, where are Holly and Vulcan?" Her Majesty asked.

"Is it not Holly's shift now," decreed the monarch. "Don't think I don't notice that you lot take it in turns to follow me around – and you, old girl, have been 'on duty' as long as I have today. I am exhausted, which means you must be very tired. Naughty Holly, she has abandoned us in our time of need. As for Vulcan, well . . . he's a law into himself. Who knows what mischief that dog is up to?"

Monty lifted his head and looked over to Candy

with an expression of shock. Candy couldn't quite believe what she was hearing, either, since it was the first time the Queen had ever spoken to them about Vulcan.

Willow knew that trouble was brewing somewhere. She could feel it in her wispy old whiskers.

"I suppose we had better put a brave face on tonight. I will have to make do with mother's tiara," Her Majesty said. "At least I have that here in the safe. Any minute now, I will need to start getting dressed and, quite frankly, I could do with a cup of tea and an early night. Come along, Monty. It's high time you did some work around here. Willow – you rest up: you are a grand old girl and you have been of great support to me in my time of need. Enjoy a long nap by the fire for the both of us, won't you?"

Willow rested her head in the Queen's soft palm. A rest in front of the fire sounded perfect.

Monty, however, was horrified. He was not accustomed to falling into any shift pattern, unlike the other dogs. He had decided long ago that he preferred to sleep for twenty-two hours of the day and use the remaining two for walks and meals.

Never before had he been asked by the Queen of England to accompany her.

Candy raised both eyebrows in mock shock and Willow yawned, grateful that someone else was taking over for the time being.

Her Majesty stood up. She looked into the large gold Regency mirror above the mantelpiece, touched the underside of her tightly curled grey hair, and said, "Right, Monty. I want you front and centre tonight. Make sure you greet all of our incredibly important Heads of State and make them feel welcome. Avoid entering into any discussions about trade negotiations, general election results, the economic situation. In fact, you'd best stay clear of anything political. Finally, Holly always gives me a signal when it's time to make my speech so if you wouldn't mind covering that tonight I'd be most grateful. Right-o let's get to work. Candy, you're up next – which dress tonight? Shoes? Gloves? Bag?"

Monty felt himself blushing with sheer panic. For the first time in his entire life he felt an odd sense of duty and hoped that wherever Holly was she would hurry up and come home soon!

* * *

Drinks were being served in the State Rooms when the rest of the family began to arrive. The President of the United States was deep in conversation with the British Prime Minister. The Ambassador to India was conversing with the Indian Prime Minister and his wife.

By now Monty was utterly terrified. He puffed up his little chest and made sure his collar was straight before entering the room. His nerves were getting the better of him. The first thing he did was trip over the German Chancellor's feet.

"Our intelligence is clueless as to who is responsible for the theft," whispered the King of Denmark. "We are, of course, doing everything we can to offer our support to Her Majesty at this great time of need."

"I hear that it was an extremely well-executed plan. They are not ruling out an insider here at the palace," replied the German Chancellor.

Monty stood between them, staring upwards, listening. The King of Denmark continued. "The thing that bothers me most is all the animals that are involved. Did you hear about the crocodile and the paw prints?"

Monty's ears pricked up. He continued to listen

as other members of the party huddled together, discussing the robberies.

It was just as the trumpets sounded to hail the entrance of Her Majesty that the penny dropped. "Oh no, oh no," he muttered under his heavy moustache of white fur. "This is all my fault! I should never have told Vulcan about Princess Alice! What have I done?"

Monty found himself the focus of everyone's attention, which was not something he was used to. Long ago, he had enjoyed being petted but now that he was older he just wanted to be left in peace. Trying not to growl, he bit his lip, and let what seemed like a hundred sticky hands stroke and ruffle his fur.

It was time for the state banquet to begin. The guests filed out of the elegant hall. Completely against normal protocol the Queen kindly insisted that Monty lead the wife of the Leader of the Free World to dinner. He walked as gently as he could for fear of running and dragging her off down the stairs.

More trumpets announced the arrival of the Queen. As the guests stood to sing the national anthem, Monty stood, with his paw across his chest, and attempted to whine along as best he could. He waited as the main course was served. All he had to do was stay awake long enough to give the Queen her signal to begin her speech. By his calculations he had been awake for over six hours, which had to be some kind of record. He stretched once, and then sat back down, running his tongue over his white moustache. The beef Wellington that was being served smelled really wonderful. He closed his eyes, savouring its smell. The combination of the warm hall, a strange rumbling from the basement and the comforting smells was all it took. Monty drifted off into an enormously pleasant, deep sleep.

22
Snorting, Chortling, Screeching and Snapping

Prince George was reunited with the rest of his family. The toddler jumped about, trying to tell his mother and Nanny all about the Line of Kings and its life-sized wooden horses. It was Princess Charlotte who spotted the old raven, sitting on the wall not far from the café. She waved at Edgar and *burbled* loudly. The Duchess saw the happy smiles on her children's faces, "Shall we go and see the raven? I have no idea where Lupo has gone, so I think a quick visit to see the birds and then we'll head home. Hopefully Lupo will be waiting for us!"

Edgar watched as the family came closer. The Princess leaned forwards in her buggy and he saw just how pretty and sweet she was. The crooked old bird's cold heart began to beat faster. There was something very special about the young royal family. For the entire time that the Duchess and her children stood talking to him, he felt extraordinary – as if being at the Tower really did matter after all.

Lupo and Holly were hiding behind the boulder. They had made a run for Traitors' Gate, only to find their exit blocked by two extremely large lizards. Looking down the narrow shaft, they could see a bat flapping away and hear the King's troops gathering. They were stuck.

Holly whispered, "Lupo, whatever happens here today, I want you to know that I am very proud of you. You tried."

"Even if it means we both get eaten?" he replied with a wry smile. Holly gave a nervous smile back, so Lupo said, "They're almost here, ready for a battle! Holly, if anything happens I want you to run as fast as you can home. I need you to protect the palace. You have to find away to block up the Black route entrance. You have to make sure the Queen is kept safe."

Holly nodded. "I will do my best, Lupo."

"No, Holly, you need to paw-promise me that

you will get away, no matter what."

Lupo knew how scared she was. "I promise," she finally replied, raising her paw and tapping it against his.

Lupo shook his head. "I'll cause a distraction." Then, looking into Holly's soft blue eyes, he said, "Holly – I'm going to go after three, OK?"

Holly nodded to show she was ready.

"One . . . two . . . three," said Lupo, then he ran out from the boulder and straight towards the fierce lizards.

Meanwhile, Holly crept out, waiting for the perfect moment to run to the doorway that led up to Traitors' Gate. The troops were getting nearer. Holly could see that they were not far off. "You need my help, you can't take these two on alone!" she shouted.

The two lizards moved into an attack position. Their strong tails flapped against the ground aggressively. The larger of them seemed very angry and moved quickly to attack.

Lupo growled, standing his ground, baring his teeth. Holly was amazed – Lupo had the two lizards' full attention. Carefully, she inched her way closer to the door. She felt like she was playing the most perilous game of Queen Mother's Footsteps ever.

Lupo warned the lizard closest to him, "Step back or else!" Then he barked, "Now, Holly, NOW!"

At the very same moment that Holly ran to the doorway, Lupo jumped forwards. From then on, everything felt like it was going in slow motion. Lupo watched as the larger lizard pounced and just as it did, the other lizard crashed right into it. Both lizards fought – they each wanted Lupo as their prize. The large lizard then fell – *SMASH* – on to the floor, knocking the other lizard to the ground.

It was Lupo's only chance to get out. As the two beasts tore at each other, Lupo ran as fast as he could towards the door.

Holly was free. She dived into the water and swam as hard and as fast as she could.

Lupo wasn't far behind. He was just about to jump into the cold water when he felt something grab him from behind. To his horror, the Crocodile King's entire army was staring down at him. There was a deafening noise as the army advanced, all snorting and chortling, screeching and snapping.

In no time at all, Lupo had been tied up with orange string, and the two lizards were punishing him by yanking and pulling on his binds. Lupo was upset at having been caught but happy that Holly had got out. He watched as the troops arrived at the archway and, one by one, swam out. This was it. Lupo knew that the world was about to witness a monster invasion at the Tower of London.

The Crocodile King was wearing the Imperial State Crown as he arrived at the archway. As he lifted it from his head Lupo thought he had a chance to grab it, but the string was yanked sharply back and he was pulled to the ground. He watched as the crown was placed inside a crocodile skin handbag.

"Don't want my crown to get all wet," said the King to his loyal followers. They grunted their approval as he grabbed for Lupo's bindings. The troops enjoyed watching their King bullying the royal dog. "This dog is coming with me. He'll be my pet in my new palace."

The King of the Thames was ready to take his troops up to the surface. "Dog!" he snapped at Lupo. "Don't even think about trying to swim away – my anaconda will be waiting to swallow you whole."

Ignoring the Crocodile King's warning, Lupo dived in. The water was refreshingly cool. After the heat of the nest, Lupo felt it hit him like a swim on a warm summer's day. Only this was no pleasant afternoon dip in the Serpentine. This was the beginning of the end. Opening his eyes under water, he could see a very large water snake below them, watching his every move. The King was right, escape was impossible – there was no way for him to outswim the giant reptile.

The snake wasn't moving. It seemed to be bewitched by the cold water. Lupo thought: Snakes can't stand the cold. That snake *can't* be awake. Gathering his courage, he pulled hard on the orange string. This time it snapped – and he was free.

Lupo started to swim away. The heavy Crocodile King immediately gave chase but was too heavy to keep up. Lupo pushed his way through the water. But as he pushed, the big anaconda came to life. It sprang forwards and caught his tail, followed by his back paw.

The snake yanked one of Lupo's back legs and then managed to grab the other. With both legs kicking like crazy inside its mouth, the snake was enraged. And then, with one click, it unhinged its jaw and Lupo felt himself being swallowed. He was

inside the snake's mouth – and there was nothing he could do about it.

The King watched as Holly made it to the surface and then looked down to see that the royal dog was gone. Several lizards swam down but the King snapped "Forget it – he's as good as dead. Pedro's eaten him."

Holly was free. She didn't look back because she knew she had promised Lupo that she would run. A flame ignited within her – a fight she didn't know she had. Using all her strength, she ran as fast and as hard as she could, away from the beasts as they chased her up the stairs and away from Traitors' Gate. She pushed harder and harder, her precious heart bursting every step of the way.

Lupo had given himself up to save her. It was the most noble and romantic thing anyone had ever done for her. As she ran, tears slipped off the side of her face. She had to keep going. Quietly, she let the flame of love that burned so brightly for him grow larger, hoping that he would get out of the water alive and they could be together again soon.

* * *

The Duchess was ready to go home, but Prince George was looking around for Lupo. "Dodo?"

The Chief of Police stepped in. "I'll do my best to find him, Your Highness. Why don't you head back to the Palace? If we catch up with Lupo, we'll be sure to return him to Apartment 1A."

George's baby sister gurgled merrily at the sight of her brother. She sat in her buggy, bobbing around and giggling at George's obvious misery. This had been the best day ever!

George moaned as he was lifted into his car seat. "Mummy . . . Dodo?" he moaned as he was clipped into his car seat.

"Let's head home – I'm sure he'll come back," said the Duchess hopefully, as she walked around to the driver's side. "He's just a bit busy right now." But as she climbed in, she did a double take. In what seemed like a fraction of a second, she could have sworn that she'd seen a crocodile running past the car wearing the Imperial State Crown.

She shook away the idea, thinking she must just be very tired. "Nanny, I have absolutely no idea what is happening today. This has to be one of the strangest days I have ever had!"

23
Let the Battle Commence

Lupo was hanging on to the inside of the anaconda's mouth, which – as it turned out – wasn't as easy as he'd have liked. Not only was it the tightest of spaces, it was also the most precarious. One slip and he would be constricted and lost for ever. Herbert had once taught him that snakes liked having their throats tickled. He decided to tickle its tonsils and see if it might help.

As he started to go to work, the snake began to giggle. To Lupo's surprise the anaconda opened its mouth as it laughed. Lupo tickled its throat as much as he dared until the opportunity arose to leap out. He took it! Swimming away as quickly as he could, he thought, Phew! It would have taken days for him to digest me and that would not have been at all comfortable!

Lupo heaved his wet body on to the staircase at Traitors' Gate and shook himself. 'Holly, I hope you got out!' he said to himself.

But there was no sign of her – the only thing he could see was a trail of slimy footprints leading towards the dungeons. Still, at least there was time for him to race to the Black route and try and stop the invasion. He ran as fast as his wet and slimy paws could carry him towards the dungeons.

Hundreds of people had arrived at the Tower to see if they could spot the Duchess and her children, and news crews and police swarmed all over the inner courtyard.

Edgar was floating. "Did you see that little girl, Claw?"

"But I thought you . . ." Claw was more than a little bit confused.

"I had the royal family all to myself. You should have heard how nice they were about the work I do here at the Tower. I'm telling you – they knew how important I was. How hard I work!"

Claw rolled his eyes. "Erm, sir, you might want to see this . . ."

Edgar pushed the rat out of the way. "What is it now?" he said as he looked out of the cell and down to the courtyard. Far below, he could see the Crocodile King and his army running towards the dungeons.

"Claw – why is the invasion happening without us?!" he exclaimed angrily.

Claw shrugged his shoulders. "Dunno," he replied.

"GET AFTER THEM!" demanded Edgar.

Herbert was watching events unfold from HQ. He ran from screen to screen shouting orders at his best agents. "Seal the Black route! All agents, do you read me? Shut the route! Let nothing through! You thought Kitty was bad, just think what it will be like having a crocodile roaming around! HURRY."

Hundreds of mice from every nook and cranny of Buckingham Palace made their way down to the entrance of the Black route. They carried with them arms made of anything they could grab. They mounted up and aimed their weapons at the fireplace, barely speaking in anticipation of the dreaded invasion.

Meanwhile, the army was forcing its way through the cobbled narrow corridors in the dungeons. The ghosts shook their chains in horror as the army moved harder and faster led by the Crocodile King.

Holly had made it all the way into the Black route. As she ran down it she barked, "Nero! Please, Nero! I need your help!"

The friendly lion appeared once again like a mist. "Holly you're alive . . . But how did you escape the crocodile and his nest?"

Holly shook her head. "There's no time to explain. I need your help – *they* are coming."

Nero roared. Ghostly animals walked out of the portraits on the walls. Then Nero asked her, "Tell me how many monsters are coming and we will try to defend you long enough for you to get to the safety of the palace."

Holly tried to fight back her tears, "Nero, I'm sorry – I think it's *all* of them."

The ghostly animals floated around unhappily. The greyhound sisters were next to speak up. "We can't possibly defend the route against an entire army of those monsters."

Annabel the royal Pekinese stood tall. "We will fight for Holly. We fight for *all* of us – everyone who was captured and taken by those wicked creatures. We use the power of our numbers. We can defeat them."

Lupo had caught up. As he rounded into the dungeons he hoped that Holly had made it to the top of the Black route and that George was safe. Herbert would send help – of that he was sure: the MI5 mouse had never let him down. As he ran, he knew he'd need all the friends he could get.

The door to the Black route was open. He watched as the water drained into it. He took one big gulp of air and jumped in. It was now or never. The small space was full of water. It took all his might to close the hatch but he managed it. The water began to subside and he found himself back in the spooky tunnel. This time he was alone. Somewhere in the distance he could hear the monsters trooping along, no doubt led by the evil Crocodile King.

He decided to try and catch up with the terrifying army. That way, he could attack from the rear. As he got closer to the troops he could hear the beast's claws, scratching at the walls and tearing the paintings of the Tower's lost animals to pieces. Soon enough, he was passing by the broken, damaged portraits scattered all over the floor. The faces of the animals looked blankly out from their frames. It was as if the very life that was once captured within the portraits had now gone.

Not too far in the distance, Lupo could see the backs of the reptiles as they moved like a wave. He prepared himself for battle.

Just as he dived forwards on his front paws, the inexplicable happened. A huge grizzly-bear ghost ran right through him. With its enormous arms and legs, and claws and teeth, it swung at the army, sending the monsters crashing to the floor like skittles. Lupo could hear the King of the Thames shouting to his troops: "HOLD YOUR GROUND! THEY ARE GHOSTS – THEY CANT HURT US!" Then the King shouted a loud but clear: "OUCH! SCRAP THAT. THEY *CAN* HURT US?!"

Lupo fought alongside the giant grizzly bear. With every swipe they both managed to regain ground. More ghosts started to appear through the walls. It looked like every animal that had ever been imprisoned at the Tower and all the animals that had once belonged to London's first Zoo all wanted to help stop the invasion.

A polar bear holding the banners of King Henry VIII ran through, sending the army running in all directions. Peacocks and tigers pecked and grabbed at the rattled reptiles. Elizabethan dogs in smart, ruffled collars barked and chased the monsters into the jaws of a pack of ghostly African lions. Lupo watched as the friendly ghosts attacked in wave after wave.

Holly was guarding the top of the route. Behind her was the entrance to Buckingham Palace. Nero was standing alongside her. His plan was working. The monster's invasion was being restrained.

"Nero, the Crocodile King was the thief," she cried. "He was the one who stole all of the jewels. He even has the Imperial State Crown. We can't let him get in. If he does he'll take the throne – he'll attack everyone in the palace."

From where Holly was standing the ghosts were winning. The King's army wildly attempted to wipe out the apparitions.

* * *

Vulcan was in the palace, checking that the monsters would have complete access. Carefully, he opened locked windows and doors. He moved furniture and triple-checked that every member of the household staff was busy overseeing the Heads of State dinner. He didn't want anything getting in the way of his plans.

Vulcan decided that this was perhaps the most despicable thing he had ever done but – at the same time – the most clever. Making the crocodile believe he was a friend had been easy. As it turned out, all he had to do was remind the beast that Princess Alice had flushed him away. Then he had suggested that King and his army invade the palace. Stealing all the jewels had also been Vulcan's idea. Managing to rob the Jewel House, without even being there, was a stroke of triumph. He stretched and smiled crookedly. He couldn't wait to get his paws on all of those jewels. He planned on spending them well.

But for now, there was the simple matter of getting rid of the crocodile. Vulcan felt an enormous sense of peace, just knowing that Lupo had been taken care of for once and for all. "Shame about

Holly," he said to himself as he made his way past a group of palace mice all carrying forks. He disliked the busy mice intensely but it would be impossible to run a palace of this size without them. He ran before the mice. "What are you vermin up to? Where are you going with the silverware?"

"Black route! Herbert sent out a red alert," said the pack's leader.

"HE DID *WHAT*?" groaned Vulcan loudly.

"Red alert. Apparently, there are some creatures trying to get into the palace. We've all been told to report to the basement."

Vulcan sniggered as a new plan formed in his mind. It was a gruesome plan! "You had better hurry along then. Better still, why don't I come with you?"

From the top of the stairs, Vulcan called out across the mass of mice who were ready in their thousands. Vulcan had never witnessed such an organised group of palace mice cramped together all in one place. "I am here to represent the interests of the crown, as you all know well," he said. "The nation has today been stricken by a new kind of monster who has taken all the treasures we hold most dear to us. I alone will go into the tunnel and plead with the monster to stop and leave this palace untouched." The mice looked pleased with Vulcan's plan. He continued, "Let me pass and I will cross into the route. Go back to your business. I alone shall stop this invasion."

The mice collectively considered Vulcan's plan and decided that it was a good idea. They put down their home-made weapons and headed back up to the palace to resume their normal duties.

As Vulcan went into the fireplace, Bernie was sure that he heard the royal dorgi mumble the words, "Foolish vermin."

Nero had headed into the fight to join the rest of the animal ghosts, which meant that Holly was on her own when the fireplace behind her clicked open. Vulcan stood in the middle of the entrance, blocking it from closing.

Holly felt a rage swelling within. "Vulcan, you have betrayed us all."

"How pleased I am to see you are quite well, Holly," the other dog jeered. "Would have been a shame to lose you to the crocodiles."

Holly felt more determined than ever. "Move out of the door, Vulcan. The entrance to Buckingham Palace is not open to your gang of thieves."

Vulcan stayed quite still. "Are you and your army of mice going to try and stop me?"

Holly could see a large group of mice gathering behind Vulcan. They looked very annoyed. "Um . . . YES . . . if you'd like to turn around you'll see that I have quite a large army."

But before Vulcan could turn, something poked him on the bottom. Then something *else* – this time, it was a bit harder. He turned around to see that the mice had all come back, unhappy at being duped.

Holly saw Bernie – she gave him a wink, which he returned, followed by the order: "CHARGE!"

Thousands of palace mice burst through the fireplace, forcing Vulcan to run into the heart of the Black route. Pretty soon the entire route was filled with mice, animal ghosts and reptiles.

As the battle raged on, high above the route the Queen and the Heads of State were discussing the importance of finding the nation's treasures. The soup course was being served. The American Ambassador leaned into the President of the United States and said, "My soup is moving?" as his plate jumped up and down. "No one told me there would be dancing in the basement after dinner."

The President looked very happy. "It's been years since I went to such an exciting Heads of State Dinner. A disco in a basement – how very British!"

24
Beyond Kitty's Imagination

When Kitty opened her eyes, the Lady in Blue was floating just in front of her. Her hair was flowing and the pretty blue dress with its delicate skirts seemed to move, as if underwater. It's a well-known fact that cats don't like ghosts but Kitty was captivated. There was something extra special about the beautiful lady who was trapped between this world and the next.

Kitty was trying her best to stop shaking. As far as she knew this was the closest any cat had ever come to a ghost. Even when she was roaming the palace at night she would deliberately avoid certain rooms and staircases at Kensington Palace because of the ghosts of King William and Queen Mary. She followed the ghostly woman to a fork in the now much wider passage. It was wide enough for several people, so

Kitty decided that they had to be below the palace.

The Lady in Blue spoke quietly. "Not much further. Please, you may find it more comfortable down here if you turn on the lights." She pointed to a brass knob on the wall. "Three twists to the left."

Kitty did as she was told and watched as the passageway lit up. They carried on walking for what must have been a few minutes when they came to a large, thick wooden door. The lady hovered next to it.

"We have arrived. Push the door and in you go."

Kitty was completely confused. They were definitely in a secret royal passage but there was no way that they could be anywhere near the Tower of London. They had only been walking for a few minutes. She pushed the door with her shoulder and it clicked open.

"Before you go in – if you'd please listen to me. Animals are not allowed in this part of the palace. You are the first and the last that shall ever come here. I am not sure what you think has happened or what circumstances have brought you to my door, but what you will see behind here is my secret. You can never tell anyone about it."

Kitty felt a chill run up her spine. In a sign that

she understood, she bowed her head. Then she pushed harder on the door, which opened widely. They were standing in a large room filled with glimmering jewels. The ghost moved over to another door and opened it to reveal a bathroom. Kitty looked up and could see a large white bathtub and a very old-fashioned wooden toilet. "I don't understand," she meowed.

The Lady in Blue appeared to be playing with something. Kitty watched as the ghost held her hands up to her ear and then said, "Yes, Inky, this is the very same bathroom."

Kitty was very confused. "Who is Inky, and why are we in a bathroom?"

The ghost spoke very softly. "Inky is my spider and we are here because you asked for my help."

Kitty's tail flicked unhappily. She was pretty sure she knew the answer to her next question, but asked anyway. "What is your name?"

The Lady in Blue floated towards Kitty's face "My name is Alice." She said as she glided down and sat on the side of the bathtub. "I was a princess once." The spider she had been talking to then ran out of her hands and went to sit on Alice's shoulder. "Inky's

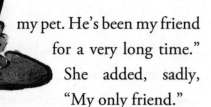

my pet. He's been my friend for a very long time." She added, sadly, "My only friend."

Kitty didn't waste a moment, "Princess Alice, my friends are in trouble. Only you can change everything."

The princess sat quietly and said, "I tried. I looked everywhere for them. I never should have put them in the toilet."

"I think you are talking about your pet reptiles," said Kitty. "Well, I think I know where they are. We just have to get to the Tower. Then you can see them for yourself – only I warn you they aren't very happy about being flushed away."

The princess ghost was distressed. "You know where my pets are?" she asked desperately.

Kitty meowed. "Yes, I think it's your pet crocodile that has caused all the trouble."

Alice was so excited she could barely contain herself. "All this time, they have been quite well, Inky! Kitty knows where they are!" she said to her spider, who seemed to whisper back. "Inky thinks it's a good idea. We will take you there."

"Alice, just quickly, may I ask how you came to be in the Keeper's Lock?"

Alice grew quiet again. Then she began her sad story. "I made a promise to never touch my mother's jewellery. Only one day, I took a diamond out to examine it. I was playing with my pet crocodile at the time. The naughty thing went and swallowed the diamond whole! You see, my pets really liked to be dressed up in fine necklaces and jewels. I tried everything to get the diamond back. I even tried bathing him with the others – that's when I flushed them all down the toilet by accident. I broke two promises that day: the first was to my mother and the second was to my pets. I promised to take care of them. So for all eternity I stand guard over the royal jewels and I will never stop until I find my lost pets."

"Seems like a lonely punishment," said Kitty sympathetically.

Princess Alice stood up, "I can't promise you that I can save your friends but I will try and make this better."

25
Bright Light

Lupo was amazed to see how scared of the palace mice the reptiles were. They fled in droves. But the battle was far from over. All around him ghostly animals continued to attack the reptiles that kept on coming. The polar bear was near him and it seemed to be managing to help keep back the larger beasts. Amongst them was the King of the Thames and Vulcan.

Lupo was exhausted. As the fighting raged on, the great battle to hold the Black route took its toll. Mice could be seen limping and being carried back to the entrance to the palace. Lupo helped to carry several mice to safety. As he carefully passed the injured mice through the fireplace that led into Buckingham Palace he spoke to Holly. "We have to stop this – I'm not sure for how much longer the mice can keep fighting."

Holly was in complete agreement, so they discussed a way to evacuate all the mice and barricade the fireplace. They both stopped when they saw Kitty walking amongst the damaged mice. Lupo and Holly were delighted to see their friend.

"So you thought you would take on a load of reptiles without me!" Kitty purred. She watched as several mice staggered by. "Looks like my new friend and I have arrived in the nick of time."

Lupo looked behind Kitty but couldn't see anyone. "New friend?" he enquired.

Kitty's eyes followed a strange misty vapour that poured into the route. Holly felt freezing cold. Absentmindedly, she moved closer to Lupo.

Nero, sensing something was happening, made his way back to Holly, calling to his troops to follow him. "Everyone – quick! Back to the fireplace!" he roared.

The King of the Thames and Vulcan took the opportunity to move closer to Buckingham Palace but were stopped by an invisible barrier.

The Lady in Blue stood charge now. All the animals ceased what they were doing and watched as the ghost made her presence known. "STOP THIS!" she commanded. "Who is responsible for this mess?"

Vulcan pushed through so that he was right in front of the princess. "You have no right to be here. You are a human ghost. I don't know who you think you are but this is . . ."

Princess Alice wasn't listening to Vulcan, although she was busy searching the faces of the reptiles in front of her. "Where are you?" she cried.

The Crocodile King pushed several lizards aside to see what all the fuss was about. When he saw the ghostly Princess Alice he stood rooted to the spot.

"Croc, is that really you?" she asked as she drifted closer towards the terrible crocodile. "It *is* you. I thought I'd lost you for ever."

Lupo watched, but the crocodile neither moved nor spoke.

Princess Alice was close enough to touch the old monster. "I have been looking for you all for so long. I have searched everywhere."

Still the crocodile did not move.

"I am *so* sorry. I never meant to flush you away.

It was an accident," she pleaded with the beast.

Lupo wasn't sure, but he could have sworn he saw a single tear roll down the crocodile's face.

Then the Black route filled with bright light. All the ghosts within it stood together. Lupo watched as, one by one, they began to disappear. The Crocodile King ordered his troops to withdraw. Vulcan sneered as he looked around, desperate for some kind of protection as the princess and crocodile walked away together.

"Kitty . . . how?" Lupo asked the palace cat.

Kitty purred with satisfaction. "I think those two have a lot of catching up to do."

Vulcan tried to run after them. "STOP – what are you doing? We are so close! What about the CROWN!?" But it was no use.

Lupo watched as the King took off the Imperial State Crown and put it to one side.

Vulcan ran and snatched it off the ground. "It's mine. MINE!" he shouted.

"No, it's not," Edgar said, appearing next to Odin and Thor. "Grab that crown, boys." He watched as the two ravens hopped on to Vulcan's back and removed the crown in one quick manoeuvre, as if they were plucking a ribbon from a child's hair. Edgar stood guard over the crown.

Lupo watched as Vulcan tried to battle with Edgar. It was no good. The raven, who was almost as big as the royal corgi, swung away and left the dog standing, looking alone and afraid.

"Now, what do I do?" Vulcan asked Lupo and Holly.

Holly turned to Nero and thanked him for helping them all. Then she walked over to Vulcan. "You come home and try your best to fit in and stop trying to take over the throne."

Vulcan was not about to agree with Holly but he knew that he had failed this time. As he walked towards the entrance at Buckingham Palace he swung his head towards Lupo. "*You* didn't win. You lost. The whole city is out of control. The nation's treasures are still in the nest with the King. I succeeded in showing the world what animals are capable of."

Edgar shook his head. "Oh, Vulcan, you still don't get it, do you? The world is a very large place and all we can do is play our part. We animals are not meant to rule. Do you really want to live the rest of your life as a miserable outcast?"

Vulcan couldn't argue with the raven. So with one last sniff of the Imperial State Crown, he pushed his way past Edgar and Holly and made his way back into the fireplace at Buckingham Palace.

Edgar waited until Vulcan had gone. Then he hopped over to Lupo and Holly. "See that this gets back to where it belongs," he said, dropping the Imperial State Crown at their paws. He ordered Odin and Thor to follow him back to the Tower. "The deed is done. We have all learnt a great deal today." With that, he hopped away.

Holly secured the Imperial State Crown to the top of Lupo's head. It was quite heavy but it seemed to sit very well on the royal spaniel. "It suits you," she said, dusting off a bit of dirt from the crown's velvet cap.

Lupo didn't tell Holly but the minute she put it on top of him he felt a strange tingling down his spine. "Erm thanks, we'd better get going," was all he could muster.

Just as they were making their way out of the Black route, Herbert raced in. "Have I missed it all?"

"YES!" Holly and Lupo said, laughing as the little

mouse shook.

"Well, then . . . that's very good . . . in fact that's EXCELLENT! I see that at least we have the crown and you'll both be pleased to hear that George is safe and back at Kensington Palace with his sister."

Lupo could have jumped for joy, if it hadn't been for the responsibility of his new job of protecting Her Majesty's crown. "Herbert, that's fantastic news. Thank you."

Kitty yawned. "Now, can we *please* go home – I have some serious sleep to catch up on!"

Herbert was less enthusiastic. "Kitty, you and I need to have a chat about boundaries . . . I must . . ."

Lupo watched as the cat and the mouse headed into Buckingham Palace.

26
A Way Home

Sometime later, Herbert, Holly, Kitty and Lupo were walking along the Red route headed for Kensington Palace. Lupo could still feel his heart racing as he walked alongside his friends. He couldn't wait to see George and Charlotte. The royal children would be thrilled to hear about being inside the crocodile's nest, the giant water snake's mouth, the animal ghosts *and* everything else that had happened. "I think George might have a hard time believing this story. This has been one awfully big adventure," he said.

Holly was sad. She could feel the weight of the world on her stout shoulders. "Lupo, this was much more than we have ever been through . . . I was very scared I'd lost you."

Lupo stopped walking and laughed. "Holly,

haven't you heard? Spaniels, especially royal spaniels, have at least nine lives!"

But Holly wasn't amused. "Lupo, I'm serious. How would I have explained it to Prince George if his best friend had been swallowed by a giant snake? Or that you had been eaten by a Crocodile King who first boiled you up in a pot of rotten mush and then used your bones for toothpicks?"

Lupo laughed. "Holly, I would always find a way home to my friends and family. Even now I know that they are in the nursery, happily waiting for me to tell them all about my adventure. Besides, the Crocodile King wouldn't have used my bones, he would have used my claws for toothpicks!"

Holly still looked sad, however, so Lupo said, "Look, let's forget about it all for a minute and go and have some fun. Do you know what I think you need? Something that's going to make you feel better. Come on. If we hurry we can still catch a few."

Holly was mystified. "Catch a few *what*? What are you talking about?" she stammered.

"You'll see. This way, come on! Kitty and Herbert can find their own way home!" With that, he ran off in the direction of Kensington Gardens. "Hurry up, old girl!"

"Who are you calling an old girl? I'll have you know that I can run almost as fast as a lion!" Holly said, racing ahead then turning back to Lupo shouted. "Be careful – you won't have any lives left if you damage that crown!"

Claw resented being summoned, particularly today. Because the Tower was so busy, the litter pickings were some of the best they had ever had. This afternoon alone he had managed to eat an entire sandwich, two large fluffy cupcakes and half a bright-green ice cream. Sucking in his large, round belly he waited for Edgar to begin.

The raven proudly pondered. "Claw, this has been one of the greatest days of my life. Alas, I don't have you to thank."

Claw looked most frustrated. "But we didn't make it to the top of the food chain – those humans are still in charge! How come you're so happy?"

Edgar clucked his beak against his wings. "I showed them – that's what! Without me here protecting their precious Tower, they will lose everything!"

"But they did lose everything," said Claw, totally confused.

"Yes, yes but they will get it all back – you'll see to that. The point is that they learnt a lesson today. A very important one."

"They did?" questioned Claw.

"Yes, they learnt that animals deserve respect. If you abandon them they will steal all your treasure!" replied Edgar righteously, bouncing around in his cell.

"I'm not sure I understand," Claw began. "I risked my life when you flew down that shaft and told the Crocodile King to steal the crown jewels – I had to rescue you! I could have been eaten by one of those loathsome monsters."

Edgar hopped around, waving his wings about as if conducting a large orchestra. "I played them all! I am a genius. Oh, what a genius I am."

"Argghh, but if you're such a genius how are you planning on getting all the rich stuff back to where it belongs?" Claw said smugly.

Edgar had a plan

for everything. "My dear Claw. You don't think I was going to let that creature have all my jewels, did you? They belong here at MY TOWER. Getting them all back well . . . that's where you come in."

"Me?" Now Claw was really befuddled.

Edgar's beak was millimetres from Claw's ratty nose. "Yes, well, you and your family and several thousands of their friends odd . . ."

Claw was not impressed. "Not again. You didn't pay them for the last removal you did! How am I meant to get them to do it again?"

The King of the Thames was sitting on the edge of one of the stones from Stonehenge. "I still don't understand why everything has to go back?" he said to the large black rat with the clipboard.

"Sorry, sir, just following orders. If you have a complaint, I suggest you take it up with management. I can give you an address if you like?" The rat handed a slim white business card to the Crocodile King. "Write a letter and pop it in the Royal Mail. They're pretty good at making sure the post gets about, even for us animals."

"But I've never posted a letter before," replied the

Crocodile King.

Ignoring him, the rat shouted out his orders. "YOU LOT, GET A MOVE ON. I'M NOT PAYING YOU OVERTIME. I WANT THIS LOT BACK WHERE IT BELONGS BEFORE MIDNIGHT."

One large rat was standing in front of Nelson "Sir, how on earth are we meant to get him back to where he belongs?"

Monty was woken up with a jolt. A hard plastic object hit the side of his head. It was a Hoover. The palace housekeepers were hard at work clearing up after the state dinner. As the monstrous machine whirled back and forth he heard them talking.

"Quite a speech she gave. The funny thing was, she normally does her speeches between courses four and five. I have never known her to leave it until course eight. I'd bet this Hoover that someone forgot to tell her when it was time."

Monty gasped. Bolting for the door, he thought the safest place for him would be the King's study but as he shot in he saw that Vulcan was already there and, rather oddly, he was sitting in Monty's warmest chair reading a book on England's maritime history with a devilish look in his eyes.

As the clock struck ten, the last of the housekeepers turned out the lights to the large hall and shut the door. Behind the door, the mice that had been hiding within the table at the state banquet got a chance to stretch their legs and hand in their notes for Herbert. On the main staircase and along the corridors, palace mice scuttled out of their hiding places and got to work. Keeping the palace in perfect order was a big job.

Upstairs, the Queen was awake. Behind her big-rimmed glasses she wore a look of concern as she sat on the side of her bed with Willow and Candy. Holly was still missing. "Well, Willow, if she isn't back by morning we will have to send out a search party. I'm just not myself without her. I never quite imagined how much I needed my Holly until tonight. Monty, I am afraid, was quite useless. I think the entire Hall heard him snoring all the way through my speech. It was most inappropriate. There is no point mincing my words. That corgi is only good for sleeping," she said, lifting her mother's tiara off her head. She sat looking in the mirror at the blank space above her head. "We'd better get another crown arranged tomorrow. I'm really not me without it, am I?" she said.

Herbert was looking at a stack of paperwork on his desk. The investigations teams had put together some pretty comprehensive reports and all of them needed his recommendations. He called for his number two to bring him in an iced bun and a fresh cup of tea.

A kindly agent brought him his snack and put it next to the files on his desk.

"Thank you, No. 2. Any news?" Herbert asked, distractedly.

"Yes, sir. The jewels have all been returned to the jewel house," No. 2 answered confidently.

Herbert almost spat all of his tea out. "They have?! Who by?"

No. 2 handed Herbert a clean handkerchief from his pocket so that the Head of MI5 could mop up his desk. "You'll have to see it to believe it, sir."

"Why's that?" Herbert asked excitedly.

"Well, sir, it was Vulcan," replied No. 2.

Herbert ran into mission control and asked to

review the tape of the crime scene. Sure enough, there was Vulcan instructing the blackest of rats on how to put back each piece.

"*The true thief at the Tower returns everything!*" Herbert said with a big smile. "I can almost see the headlines now."

27
A Twinkling Crown

The Duke was pleased to get some fresh air. It had been a long night. The park was completely empty. Since the gates were locked he was able to walk without being disturbed.

Prince George and Princess Charlotte had made a dreadful mess of the nursery after they had returned from the Tower. He had spent the rest of the afternoon building dens and pretending to be Lupo hiding in corners from Nanny and the Duchess.

A pair of dogs barked in the distance and his thoughts immediately turned to the royal spaniel. He wished his dog would come home soon. He knew that Lupo liked having an adventure or two but he'd been gone for a long time.

The Duke walked further into the park. The dogs

he could hear seemed to be having a very good time. Three squirrels dashed past him in a big hurry. The Duke's eyes narrowed. "It can't be!" he said.

Lupo saw the Duke before the Duke saw Lupo. Their game of chasing squirrels was finished. "You see, Holly. Sometimes you just have to not be a royal dog and just focus on being a normal dog," he barked.

"LUPO! HOLLY! COME HERE AT ONCE!" shouted the Duke, running into the middle of the Park. Then he saw something he recognised. "WHAT IS THAT YOU ARE WEARING . . . OH MY . . ."

The Duchess received a call from the Duke that he had found Lupo and that their spaniel was wearing the Queen's crown. She immediately told the children, who both leapt happily up and down. She was still smiling when the Duke walked in to the kitchen at Apartment 1A carrying Holly under one arm and the Imperial State Crown in the other. Lupo walked beside him and was clearly looking very pleased with himself.

"I have no idea how he did it, but our dog got my grandmother's crown back," said the Duke.

His wife clapped her hands in delight. "What a

clever thing you are, Lupo!" she said, as she bent down to pat his head. "Looks like you had some help. Hello, Holly," she said, smiling at the Queen's favourite corgi.

"It baffles me," replied the Duke, shaking his head. "How did they get out? How did he get the crown? And what is that dreadful smell?"

From the kitchen the Duchess could hear her children shouting with glee. She smiled. "I think they'd like to see Lupo before bathtime."

Lupo didn't wait to be called. He ran as fast as he could all the way to the nursery. Bursting in, he bounded into Prince George's arms and then right into Princess Charlotte's bouncer.

"Dodo!" screamed the Prince and Princess together.

The Duke and the Duchess watched as Holly joined in, giving the royal children lots of licks and cuddles.

Lupo barked, "It's great to be home. Guys, I have the best story for you! Holly and I had the biggest adventure. Do you want to hear all about it?"

"YES! YES! YES!" yelled the children.

Prince George gave his friend a big squeeze and

gurgled in their own secret language. "I knew you would make it home, buddy."

Hearing all the noise, Nanny walked in to investigate. "What on . . . LUPO . . . You're home. Oh, that's wonderful. Hang on – what's that stench?!"

The Duke and the Duchess said it together. "Bubble crown!"

Nanny looked less than impressed. "Looks like we are going to be giving everyone a bath together tonight. I'd better get my super bubbles out if you are all going to be playing bubble crown."

Prince George was still hugging Lupo when he said, "I can make the biggest crown using bubbles!"

Lupo licked the side of his best friend's face. "Bet mine will be bigger!"

With that, the two friends ran all the way to the bathroom. Holly looked up at the Princess and smiled. "Well, Charlotte, shall we see how we can get on?"

Holly was surprised when the princess *cooed*, "Yes, please, Holly – finally it's good to have someone understand me!"

As the entire family played happily in the bathroom none of them saw the ghost of Princess

Alice floating through to the kitchen, and over, the dirty Imperial State Crown with its missing emerald.

"You want to be careful with that, it's the only one," said Kitty, watching from the kitchen worktop.

Princess Alice raised a finger to her pale lips and swapped the crown for a shiny new one. She whispered to the palace cat, "Shh. Remember it's our secret."

Kitty watched as the lady drifted away with the old crown and then stretched. "I have three days until the Duke's brother returns from Africa – and no matter what happens, NOTHING is getting me out of bed!" With that, she sauntered out of the kitchen and up the stairs to Apartment 2.

The other pigeons in Trafalgar Square stared at Johnny who was still sitting on Lord Nelson's shoulder, not moving a muscle.

"How long has he been like that?" asked Jonny, another pigeon.

"Do you think he's all right?" asked the pigeon's best friend, Doris.

"Well, I think I saw him blinking a minute ago . . ." said Bobby, a racing pigeon, stopping on his way to Birmingham. "But then again I could be wrong."

A white pigeon, who spent most the year trying to work out which way was north, flew down from one of the stone lions' heads and landed on top of a newspaper as it floated by.

The heading read: MYSTERY SURROUNDING RETURN OF NATIONAL TREASURES. WILL ENGLAND EVER BE THE SAME AGAIN?

The white pigeon said, "Personally, I think Jonny and Nelson look quite good on the third plinth. I'm just not sure Dippy the dinosaur belongs all the way up there on the top of the admiral's column, though . . ."

Herbert walked into his office, sat down and promptly sneezed. "No. 2, please can you get me the dustpan. I think I missed a few cat hairs . . . I honestly think I am allergic to Kitty. Either that or I caught a cold at the Tower!" He reached for the handkerchief in his pocket. But instead, he pulled out the emerald. Holding the green gem, he went to mission control and watched as the Queen walked into Parliament wearing her perfect Imperial State Crown. "Where is the missing stone?" he asked aloud.

No. 2 stood next to him holding the dustpan and brush. "Stone, sir?"

"The Lady in Blue . . ." Herbert said smiling to himself.

"Sir, can I help you with anything other than the dustpan?" asked No. 2.

"Yes, see that this emerald is taken to Kensington Palace. Tell the SAS I want it returned to the Lady in Blue immediately."

Lupo and Holly were snuggled up in the nursery. Lupo was under Prince George's bed. Holly was on top of it. They had spent the entire night playing bubble crown and telling the children all about their adventures at the Tower of London.

"Leave the dogs – they look shattered," said the Duke. "I'll take Holly back to the palace tomorrow. They must have had one incredible adventure."

At that moment, the Duchess heard

the phone ringing, so she left her family and went to answer it. Five minutes later, she returned to the nursery to find the Duke fast asleep on the little blue sofa. Nanny too was asleep in an armchair near the door with her knitting.

The Duchess settled herself into her rocking chair and soon fell asleep as well. It was the first night in a very log time the entire household got a good night's sleep.

Epilogue

The Crocodile King sat on the floor of his empty room. Someone knocked at the door. "What is it?" he said gruffly.

"Sir, someone has come to see you," answered the lizard.

"What do they want?" asked the miserable crocodile.

"Well, they say they want to trade. They found something you'd like."

The crocodile debated if it was worth letting the trader in. "What is it?"

"They said it was a ship."

"I don't want another ship."

"I think you might want this one," said the Lizard opening the door to let the black cat in.